Eagle Tripping Out

By Ashaki Boelter

<u>Other books that are written by Ashaki Boelter:</u>

Doomed School
Beware of a Cat's Fury
The Nok
Witch Momma, Dummy for Hire
Destined To Win
Thirst for Blood
The Bloody Curse of Humankind

By Ashaki Boelter

Eagle Tripping Out

A Novel

Ashaki Boelter

Shakalot High Entertainment

Eagle Tripping Out
Copyright © 2020
Ashaki Boelter

Library of Congress
Cataloging-in-Publication Data

ISBN: 978-1-7358905-3-1

Eagle Tripping Out

Written by Ashaki Boelter

All Illustrations by Ashaki Boelter
Printed in the USA by Lulu Publishing
Published by Shakalot High Entertainment, 2020

Edited: In-House Shakalot High Entertainment

By Ashaki Boelter

I was tripping when I wrote this.

Life happens

TABLE OF CONTENTS

By Ashaki Boelter

By Ashaki Boelter

Chapter 1

State of Shock

"My ex-wife can go to hell!"

Lester had been married to Katy for ten years, but their relationship turned severely crappy after the first. They were close initially, squeezing a little boo-boo to the mix, but they became as tight as gluteal amnesia as time went on. Numbed and sore, rather messy after the marriage honeymoon stage, and after a lot of teary swabbed tissues, several things came to their supposed rescue: Egos, evil, and a mouthful of diarrhea from Katy's people.

All three of those sinister droppings stirred into one and created a whirlwind of ego-tripping out from Katy. For Lester, to have flown above her rejection, trashy rumors, and that goldmine of a boyfriend she took up was like an eagle that landed upside down and heads first on the moon.

Just when he thought he was finally above it all, years after his divorce, Lester found that those teary issues that were once flushed came back up time and time again. His past with Katy was like a beached whale on porcelain. If it wasn't her scavenger co-workers or crappy friends that he crossed in her shithole side of town from time to time, it was the respectable glance of the little stinker born between the two that was a constant reminder of how terrible their marriage was.

"Hello, is somebody there?"

"Who in the hell is this, bro?"

"It's Lester."

"Oh, hey man, how are you doing?" It was none other than Katy's rebound king, the significant, big-old fat lover, Johannes Fujiyama. He was once the diamond and its shell of a man to the ladies at her previous job. The blubber butt slept with all of them, but in the end, it was Katy's blabbermouth about her awful marriage that got her settled with the caring gargantuan. "Lester, I almost did not recognize your voice. Do you have a bad cold or something? You sound terrible!"

"Isn't this my son's cell phone? Why do you answer it every time I call? Johannes, I'd like to speak to my son."

"Let me go and find him," replied Johannes. He quickly closed out the Internet on the phone because he had been watching porn on it before the call. "I think your son is in the john. He always leaves his phone on the couch. I would think that as a young man, he'd want to take it with him in the john. Do you know what I mean, a little pissing, some boo-booing, and then a little dice action practice with the peter? I guess he's like you and that he's not wired that way."

"Can you tell my son to call me when he's finished?"

"Wait. I think Reggie just finished! I just heard the toilet flush. He's on his way. Hold on, Lester."

"Okay."

"Damn, boy!" shouted Johannes. "Close that bathroom door! Did you spray in there? I can smell it out here! Did you eat a skunk?"

Lester was hot about Johannes talking to his son like that!

Then Johannes growled more, "Reggie, come get your narrow ass over here and answer your cell phone. It's your deadbeat dad!"

"Hello?"

"Reggie!" The happiest father on the planet welcomed his son to the phone. "How are you doing, son?"

"Dad, I miss you so much! Are you coming to my sixteenth birthday party in a few days?"

"I would not miss it for anything, son!" However, Lester had to be real about his schedule challenges that day. "I do need to attend an important luncheon in Los Angeles the night before your birthday party. I'll make it to your house at around five o'clock the next day."

"That's awesome, dad! I cannot wait to introduce you to my new friends I met while playing on the school basketball team!"

"I cannot wait. So, do you have a girlfriend now?"

"Oh yeah, you know me."

"That's my boy. What's her name?"

"Her name is Anita. She's super-smart and seriously hot! I invited her and some of her friends. Mom was against me inviting girls, but Johannes demanded it."

Johannes shouted in the background, "It ain't a party without the chicks! I don't see anything wrong with a little bump and grind."

"I look forward to meeting all of your friends *and Anita*."

"It's cool that you'll be here! I have been telling all of my friends about how cool you are. Do you have a girlfriend now, dad?"

"I try."

"It is okay, dad." Then Reggie whispered, "One of my friends has the hottest mother. I could invite her and introduce you."

Lester laughed. "Hey son, I have a few days off too after your birthday. Maybe your mom will give in a little and let me have you around my spot for a couple of days? Maybe we can drive out to Seaside or even Seattle for a few days? We can have maybe a father-son vacation."

"That would be awesome, dad!" Reggie turned to make sure his mother's boyfriend wasn't spying on his call. "I don't think she would miss me, as long as muscle-brain-ding-dong is here. I rarely see her now that he has moved in. They hardly ever leave the bedroom!"

"He moved in?"

"Yes, and he is so gross," whispered Reggie. "He walks around the house, butt-naked, all the time, and farting. I caught him in the living room, jacking off to pornography on the computer, during the middle of the night. He keeps the house smelling terrible because he cooks chitterlings every week. I don't think Johannes cleans those good enough, and he likes them so much that he adds them to smoothies; it looks like Johannes drinks poop!"

"Who are you whispering to on the phone?" asked Reggie's mother. Hunched over her son, she looked back over her shoulder and caught Johannes's attention. "Whom is Reggie talking to?"

"It's his dad," answered Johannes. He pulled a booger from his nose and rolled it in his fingers. "Hey baby, do you have any more weed? We're kind of low. I am going to have to go downtown to buy more. Um! Damn, Katy, your butt looks good in those shorts!"

"I know what you want!" Katy shook what the Lord gave her.

"Get over here and let me spank that bubble butt!"

"Mom, I am talking to dad!" Reggie was disgusted.

"What? Give me that phone!" Katy demanded. "Boy, you'd better knock that look off of your face before I— I don't care if you were not done talking to your daddy! Shut up. We're in my house, and that is my phone; I pay for the damn cell service. Thank you."

Johannes laughed at Reggie and said, "Shows you right, you little punk. If I was your mom, I'd of beat that ass. You show some respect in your mother's house! Do you understand, boy?"

"Lester?" Katy held the phone. "Hello, is this Lester?"

"Katy?"

"Well, hello there, Les." Katy calmed down.

"How have you been, Katy?"

"Not lonely." Katy wiped her bangs back and giggled. "So, are you going to make it to your son's birthday party this time? He is looking forward to seeing you. You know that you cannot let him down again."

"I know."

"You cannot keep giving broken promises! I mean… The last time, you said you'd make it to one of his basketball games, and you never showed up! You were supposed to pick him up about two weeks ago but canceled because of your job."

"I got to pay child support, so I had to."

"Lester, man, I do not want to take your sorry ass to a judge. Our divorce and child time was amicable. Do you understand? You cannot take our divorce out on our son! Step off of your shame, man. Spend time with him and come to his birthday party."

"I know, Katy. I know."

"Yeah, whatever, Lester, I also know that you cannot stand to see the sight of such a big man cuddling up with me in public places, but you're going to have to get over it. You and I are over, and that's how Johannes and I do things. If you come over to *my house*, you might even see a pair of panties or his draws lying around the house. You may even see a pair on the front lawn. We're very loving around here, unlike what you and I had."

"I think I need to go now."

"I know you, Les. I know you're hurting inside. I know you're a church-going, spiritual kind of guy. Go to God with your pains like you always have done. That is how you work. Frankly, I know that I held you back from being a preacher, but I'm not holding you back from getting laid. I found that that gets you past any ex when the getting is good."

Johannes laughed in the background. "Ask him if he knows how to fight an exorcism! He could be a priest because we all know that he's not getting any, so he's on his way! I don't know if we should leave Lester alone with your son at our house!"

Katy and Johannes were both high and laughed it up.

"What the hell, Katy!" Lester's mouth hung open. "Why would you go there? Good Lord! You know what? Look. I only called to talk to our son."

"I said all of that because *I know you,* fool. We had our day! I know you are not over me. Look. My friends saw you at the riverfront recently, looking like a reject, crying and shit. Come on, man, get over it!"

Johannes pretended to sob and added, "What a wuss! Was he out there, crying like some little punk-ass bitch? What a sissy! You'd never see me crying over a woman. Katy, you married that?"

Katy smiled and shushed Johannes. "Look, Lester, I should've listened to my father from the start. Our relationship and marriage was a nightmare the whole time. It was wrong and volatile from the start!"

"Okay, why are you still repeating that every time I call for my son? Anyways, you tell your spies to leave me alone!"

"That's so immature," replied Katy. "Here, I will put our son back on the phone before you break down crying or something. I can hear it in your shaky voice. You're such a weak, little man, but thank the Lord that you worship, that I got a real man nowadays!"

"You know what? You and that thug boyfriend of yours can kiss the blackest part of my hairy ass!"

"Hello? Dad, are you okay?"

Lester held his tongue from saying what he was about to say. "Reggie? Son, you are back on here. Thank the Lord!"

"Are you okay, dad?"

Lester thought back about why he didn't get his son two weeks ago. He claimed that he had to work twelve-hour days, but he briefly showed up at Katy's house recently. So, what was up with the excuse? Lester was not a dead-beat dad, but he had reason to welcome the title!

Two weeks ago, he pulled up to Katy's house. The first thing that happened was that he felt the earth shake while he stood on her wooden front porch. Before he knocked on the front door, he heard somebody trying to start a lawnmower at the side of the house. He figured his son was given the chore to cut the grass, so he went over there to surprise him.

Instead of telling his son that the lawnmower possibly needed some gasoline, when he peeked over the wooden gate door, he found Johannes hammering his delighted ex-wife! The thug's manhood looked like it came from an enormous Clydesdale and was surgically attached to a string bean. All that rambling motor noise was nothing more than Johannes grunting, with a mouthful of grounding golden glitter!

Lester was in a state of shock and envy as his gonads shrank to the size of a lobster eyeball. He'd forgotten about why he was there, to start. Lester turned around, got in his old car, and sped home. Lester couldn't tell his ex-wife about two weeks ago; he knew Katy had the gull to call the cops and press charges claiming he was a peeping tom. He skipped telling his son because it would've gotten back to his momma, and she would have pressed charges that he was a peeping tom.

"I'm okay, son. I'll be there for your birthday party, I promise. I may have failed at being your mother's husband, but nothing is going to stop me from being your father! I love you, son."

Suddenly Katy hollered out, "He's a liar, and he ain't going to show up! Your father is a loser, Reggie! I don't know why you're wasting your time with that sucker. Just hang up the phone and wash those dishes in the kitchen before I bust that butt! And when you're done with those, you'd better fold all the towels on the couch that I left for you. And vacuum the floor!"

"Son," stated Lester, "only the truth will set us free. Someday, you'll see me fly above it all, like an eagle, and you'll get there too."

Chapter 2

Having Too Much Fun

"Is my tie straight? How does it look? Is it okay?"

"I guess."

"That doesn't help, Gerry." It was one of the biggest nights of Lester's corporate career. The hard-working, single father was up for a prestigious award at the regional company dinner in Los Angeles. Ten minutes left before the start of the meeting, held in a popular casino's boardroom.

"You look great, Lester." Gerry marveled at his childhood friend's suit and haircut. Together, they stood at the bathroom mirror.

"Well, okay. You know, Gerry, if you had stayed around long enough, you probably could have been here with me accepting this award and all of the money awarded with the raise. I cannot believe you left this mega Fortune 500 Company to move down here to southern California to work in a small casino as a cook."

Gerry reminded his friend of how freedom looked. "Besides being the best cook in here, I make enough money with part-time hours to spend valuable time with my family! This place is built off the back of a ma and pa operation; they know how to treat employees directly and fairly. We don't feel like we have numbers on our back and can be replaced at the snap of a thumb. My job doesn't have rules on how much time can be taken off. Besides, who would want to abuse time-off when you like your job? It's not an issue here. You'd have to be a fool not to want to work here. That's why I'm here; I'm free."

"Is that right? So, you don't think that I'm free?"

"When I worked for your company, I refused to allow those corporate jerks to confuse our indigenous people's morals with their economic and capitalist plan that take away what our ancestors taught. When it comes to honesty and family, I would never again surrender life to a corporation with their two-to-three weeks off a year and pennies I would earn to a CEO's million. I'll never be used or become some company's token! Give me a ma and pa operation on any given day, where I see meaning that applies to me!"

"So, you think that a big company is using me?"

"You'll never make CEO money as long as you work there, and if you call out to spend time with your family, even if they have enough heads in the office, you'll still be disciplined or left counting your so-called earned time. You are simply owned. We're Native Americans and black, so tell me why I should allow a white corporation to own me? They stole our land, enslaved us, and now they're stealing souls from us. So tonight, go out there, show some teeth, and accept your plaque."

"Damn. Gerry, did you smoke a little weed today?"

Gerry stood to Lester's face. "Remember this, bro. When I die, I'll go with honor and with prideful ethnicity of our true people. I will not have lived a lie. Their so-called American dream of living large is a hoax. My legacy will be faithful and richest to my culture. I'd rather work three low paying jobs, to be real, than one that takes me away from our richness. We were not put on this earth to praise money and go on shopping sprees."

"It sounds as if you're calling me a sellout, Gerry."

"Do you feel like a sell-out?" Gerry puckered his lips.

"No, but all I got to say, Gerry, is that at least I attempt to make enough money to pay my child support. That's about being a man across the board. Let me accept my reward with pride."

"That's cold, you black Indian." Gerry giggled. He was guilty, though, and he knew it. Gerry had not paid child support to any of his babies' mommas, ever. That had gotten around Los Angeles; he couldn't buy a girlfriend. He donated chromosomes to create eight kids and then split to southern California. "I'm proud of you. You'd better go up there and represent. Don't forget who you are."

"I'm black and Native, and I'm proud!"

"Right on!"

By Ashaki Boelter

Lester watched his closest friend throw up a fist and noticed a tattoo he had never seen. "When did you get that cool tattoo of a vicious eagle carrying a rifle in the center, on your forearm?"

"I got it about a month ago," answered Gerry. "It represents a battle that my family had with some back-stabbing white Oregon Trail settlers that stole our food and supplies through lies and false agreements, wronged black people on our sovereign land because of the Oregon Leash Law, and raped our women. As the story went, our brave High Chief, my great grandfather, was sick of settler's big-time and conceited egos. At the same time, they labeled us as easy and primitive, that he transformed into an eagle, stole the settlers' rifles, shot them from the air, and then violently ate them all. The story is of vengeance against people, including our own, which damn or blemish our legacy and pride! You never let your ego get ahead of us, whether we walk the earth or bound to heaven."

"Not only was I unaware that you were related to the story, but I had never heard that ridiculous version of the tale growing up. What I heard was that after the eagle shot them, it then turned on us and ate our wealthiest leaders, along with their children, because they constantly stole from the poor to incite a war of responsibility. It was poor people, who had no desire to work, but the rich envied the poorer family bond, the wealthiest value in life. The poorest people wanted the wealthier people to carry on the tribal foundation, building, and feeding, to do all the work, while the poor gain from nothing. So, the eagle scared everyone to do something in life, poor or rich. Belief in the Great Eagle levels the playing ground of our people. You left a great job here because of your ego. You sinned by quitting, and the eagle is watching you."

"Get the hell out of here; I left the company because of racism. Your version of the Great Eagle is a bunch of bullshit! Who taught you that version?"

"You only stated the first part of the Great Eagle story. You need to read or hear the full story if you're going to profess the truth."

"My family wrote the full history of the eagle, Lester!"

"But there were other witnesses, Gerry! There are other interpretations, and so, there's more to it than archaic revenge. The newer interpretations explain more to what we can relate to today."

"Unlike you," replied Gerry, "I know the real truth, not opinions from outside interpretations. See, this is what I'm talking about, brother. See why I left your company? Jobs like you have, in this country, are designed to make people forget who they are. This country will strip values and lessons from us before you know it, plaguing our stories with more lies and other meanings, and we'll become ignorant and accept things like gentrification. They will turn us into their sinful ways and rid our culture for good."

"I know the truth, or my name isn't Lester Hairston, brother!"

Gerry shook his head. "I guess we can still be of the same body with different theologies. It's okay to agree to disagree, like most other subjects. At the end of our various journeys, we follow our heavy convictions. Who am I to thwart your mission to mines? I'm just a man at the end of the day."

"We all just want what's best for our peeps."

"Then you go out there and represent our people, Lester! Stand tall and know that with our people, should anyone disrespect us, we'll strike back like that eagle!"

Lester agreed. "I can receive that! Amen!"

"Your award as Employee of the Year represents our people," said Gerry. "So, get out there on that stage and thank them, but let them know who we are and what you expect. If you go out there and they later talk shit about you, we've got an eagle spirit that they can confront, so don't be fearful!"

"I'm not scared!"

"We, as a people, are strong and will never forget who we are. Don't you ever turn your back on us or talk lowly or marginalize our people, or else you can face the death of the giant eagle that always protects us, whom we believe is a gift that was given to us by God!"

"He gave us a mighty eagle!"

"Lester, you're one of the ones that made it, and I love you for that!" Gerry swept dust from Lester's shoulder. "Be brave and be you, but do not become a corporate puppet or a sellout. And most importantly, keep your ego in check."

"I appreciate that. Thank you for helping me with my tie."

"Make us all proud that an indigenous man is being appreciated. Let them know what's up!"

"Thank you, Gerry. And I will."

"Now, I am truly honored."

Suddenly, a white guy walked out of a stall, laughing. He had flushed the toilet and walked to the sink to wash shit from his fingernails. "You Indians are fucking racist! I remember you, Gerry when you worked for us. You got fired! And, I heard the story about the eagle you just told. You're on some serious drugs, man!"

Gerry shook his head. "Go fuck yourself."

For the next few bruising hours of the meeting, the company's Chief Operating Officer and CEO went over the yearly budget and goals of Valuable Marketing Corporation. The introduction of new business partners was revealed. The annual percentages of losses and gains were released. Overall, the company was nowhere near folding, and big banks supported their goals.

"This employee has shined for years, and it is time to give him the attention he has earned and deserves," said the CEO at the podium. "Let us give a warm appreciation to the Employee of the Year, who has the highest client base and the most funds coming in from his successful portfolio, Lester Hairston! Come on up here, son!"

"Thank you all," said Lester. He stood at the microphone in front of all staff, corporate giants, and business partners. Then he pulled a piece of paper from his pants pocket and proceeded to read his prepared speech.

Five minutes later…

"…So, in conclusion," Lester wrapped up, "I want to thank all of my constituents that helped prime me for such an honor. Lord knows that I've had many distractions with life in general, but the love from the company I get has always been consistent. It is such an honor. Thank you, and let's make the next fiscal season rock! And remember to keep your eyes on the prize like eagle eyes on a rodent! That is what I do, and I will continue to do so. Thank you all!"

The room erupted in a hazy shade of cheers!

"That was an unbelievable speech!" jeered Rhonda Patterson. She had strategically found a way to find a seat at the very same table as Lester. Everyone knew Rhonda, especially the men in the company. She was restroom conversation daily for men. She was the biggest flirt in history! "You are so presidential and sexy, like President Barack Obama! Has anyone ever told you that?"

"No."

"You look just like him too."

"You don't say?"

"You have so much potential!" Rhonda gasped and giggled. She worked on Lester tonight and had not begun at the table. Last week, in the company elevator, she snapped a picture of his behind on her cell phone and vowed to grab it someday.

"Thank you for the compliments, Rhonda."

"Before I forget, I was wondering if you wouldn't mind coming to a party that I am throwing for a friend in Tacoma next week. I kind of heard about your divorce from a mutual friend, and I have a girlfriend that may be interested in a blind date."

"Is she cute?"

"Of course, she is! She is so ready to settle down; she is looking for a good time with a good man that has his shit together. What do you say? Are you interested?"

"Sure! I would be delighted to meet her."

"I was also wondering about tonight." Rhonda sipped on her wine and tongued her lips. "You know, Lester, I am not about to sell my friend a lemon. I do like to test drive things before I sell them to a potential buyer. Do you understand what I'm saying?"

"Excuse me!" Suddenly, Gerry showed up and stood behind Lester. "I just want to shake your hand! I am proud of that speech you gave. That was awesome, Lester!"

"Thank you."

Gerry placed his hand on Lester's shoulder and sat a massive bottle of alcohol in front of his buddy. "It is on' the house. So, who is this beautiful woman at the table across from you? She is quite the vixen!"

"Gerry, this is Rhonda. And Rhonda, this is Gerry, who is one of my best friends from Oregon. He works and lives around here now. He used to work with this company a long time ago."

"You work here? That's cool, but you say that you live around here?" Rhonda asked.

"Yes."

"There's not a nice neighborhood in at least ten miles from here. How did you end up living in a nasty area around Los Angeles? I would've stayed in Portland! Unless you're a professional basketball player or an actor, why would you live here?"

"Firstly, I'm not originally from Portland," answered Gerry. "I moved there and did my senior year of high school there, but all of my other years I lived around or in Warm Springs. I moved to Los Angeles, I guess, to have fun! I like it here."

"There guess there is nothing wrong with that!" Rhonda nodded. She continued to talk about what was fun to her, from amusement parks to movie locations. To no avail, Rhonda hadn't noticed that Gerry was fixed on her breasts. Her oily double-D breasts nearly flopped out of her top and onto the table, should she have eaten one more bite of food.

"Whatever, lady, it has been my greatest pleasure to meet you. Can I get you anything from the kitchen? Any friend of Lester is a friend of mines. I can see that he has great taste!"

"Thanks, Gerry," chuckled Lester. "Look, man, we will hook up after my job dinner meeting is over. Put your tongue away."

"Are you trying to get rid of me?" Gerry then laughed. "I'll see you then, player. We can open that bad boy up and get drunk!"

"Hold on there, Lester," said Rhonda. "How are you going to hook up after this dinner with him? I am over here because I was trying to ask you for a ride home. After all, my ride left early to deal with her kids at her hotel. They are fighting, I guess. You know how kids can be. You cannot leave them alone for that long."

"Ah, man," moaned Gerry. He had a massive smile on his face and patted Lester on the back. "Dude, you had better think about taking the gal back to her hotel! I can understand that responsibility! I'd take a rain check unless she got some friends I can hang with?"

"It is late, Lester," added Rhonda. "I was wondering if instead of sitting any longer in this meeting, you and I could sneak away."

"He is going to get some of that," moaned Gerry. He watched his friend and Rhonda leave the room.

The night was young, and Lester escorted Rhonda to his ride.

"You drove that old car from Oregon, and it made it here in one piece?" asked Rhonda. "Are you serious?"

"It is a classic!" Lester was proud of his ride. "I put a lot of money into the engine. And, of course, it made it. I'm here, ain't I?"

Once she was inside his car, Lester entered the driver's side and proceeded to start it.

Chug-chug-chug! Chug-chug!

"What's wrong with your car, Lester?"

"I don't know. I think the starter may have gone out. It could be a water pump. Just stay right here. I'll be right back, Rhonda."

The fact was that Lester ran out of gas, but he did not want Rhonda to know of his idiocy. So, he sprinted into the casino's restaurant kitchen.

"Gerry, I need your help! Gerry!"

"You're still here?" asked Gerry. "You have a fine woman in your car, bro! What in the world are you doing back here?"

"I need your vehicle, bro! My car is out of gas. Look, man, I'll take her back to her hotel and then bring your car back when I'm done. Just give me about two hours."

Gerry handed over his keys. "No problem. It is the lime-green truck out back with a homemade wood camper on the back."

"Are you for real?"

"Give me the keys to your car. I'll have it filled before you get back in the morning."

"Now, wait a second. I will not be out all night with her!"

"Man, you take my truck and enjoy the drinks I have in the back cooler. You rock that fine ass chick to the break of dawn. If you cannot make it to the hotel, feel free to park at a rest stop and set it off! My truck is good for camping. I should know. If you can't wait, you can find a dark corner in the casino parking lot. None of the cameras are working anymore. Just duck the occasional security officer. That's what I do! And I have plenty of clean sheets in the back, bro."

Lester returned to his car but saw Rhonda walking away. She was on her cell phone and called for a ride-share to take her back to her hotel.

"Wait! Rhonda, I got a ride, so hang that up. Follow me!"

"I was worried that you weren't going to return," said Rhonda. "I figured that you caught shaky knees, you know. I am coming at you kind of fast and all. I know you are recently divorced. I understand if you need more time. I was there before too."

"I am fine, Rhonda. I will be using my friend's truck to take you back to your hotel or to wherever you so desire. The company said they would take care of my car repairs tonight."

"Wow! You are like mister big now."

"You know, what can I say? I am the Employee of the Year."

"Wait a second. Lester, why are you stopping in front of this green, homeless shelter on wheels?"

"It is not a shelter. It's a truck! It is my friend's ride, so get your hot booty inside."

"I am not riding in that piece of shit! Are you crazy?"

"Hell, yes!" Lester opened the door for her and watched her get inside the truck. He closed her door and hopped into the driver's side door. He pulled out his bottle of wine, given as a gift from Gerry. "I think if we take a couple of drinks of this, sooner or later, this truck will feel like a big SUV."

"I don't want to drink from the bottle like some wino! Take me to my hotel so that we can have a romantic glass and whatnot."

"You're right," replied Lester. "Let's get moving. You're staying where I am, at the Blue Lemieux Hotel, right?"

"Yes."

"Ewe, ah yuck, it stinks in here like old, cheesy broccoli and dirty socks! And is that a used condom on the floor mat?"

"Is it?"

"Let me out of here, Lester! I'll call a cab or something. Open this door! It's jammed. I want to leave now! I'll break a window if you don't let me out of here."

"Fine then," said Lester.

Just as the Employee of the Year opened his door, Rhonda grabbed a handful of his sleeve. "Wait!"

"What?"

"Drive this truck, Lester. Come on! Drive!"

"You wanted to leave, but now you want me to drive?"

"He's coming this way!"

Lester was like, "Who?"

"The CEO is coming this way. Oh, my god. His car is parked right next to me! He cannot see me in here with you because of our company policy. I am a manager, and I cannot be caught associating with employees under me, even if you're in a different department."

"I'm the Employee of the Year; that should mean something!"

"That ain't anything but a few extra cents earned. So, step on the gas quickly! Drive, man! Go!"

"First, I want you to kiss me." Lester started the truck. "Forget about all of those company policies. I want at least a kiss like you were about to give me. I see where this is going now!"

"What? We have to go! Come on!"

"Kiss me, and then I'll—,"

"Come here, Lester!"

Rhonda and Lester's lips abruptly connected, their mucus tongue splashed into one other's gums and jackhammered dinner remnants like a blender of butterscotch rice pudding. After flossing and tongue wrestling, they backed away and wiped their mouths.

"That was incredible, but you get us the hell out of here!" Rhonda dove onto Lester as he backed the truck out of the parking lot. He scraped a couple of parked cars and set off car alarms. Rhonda was turned on by danger, unbuckled his pants belt, and licked all over his hairy body. Blame it on the alcohol, but she majorly influenced the way he drove tonight, as he sped out of the parking lot and dinged a few parked cars on track to ecstasy!

After Lester successfully drove them away from the parking lot, he rumbled across the nearby highway's meridian and crashed through bushes! They rolled into a rest stop parking lot, drove over a handicap parking block, and stopped in front of the restroom door.

Soon after, they finished off the bottle of wine. Then Lester and Rhonda crawled into the back of Gerry's truck, found more drinks and a bag of trees, and rolled around the sheets, caressing and sucking. They got so drunk and high that they humped each other's brains out with laughter and harmony. After sensational drenched relief, they passed out.

The next morning had come. Rhonda awoke, upside down, in the driver's seat of Gerry's truck, which was now parked in front of Gerry's casino job.

"Lester?" Rhonda turned right-side-up and looked everywhere in the truck. He wasn't upfront with her, and she couldn't make out the lumps of blankets in the back. "Oh, my god, Lester, you got the best of me last night. You make me want to be demoted to a regular employee! Where are you, Lester? Are you in the back? I don't remember much about what we did, but I feel so good. Lester?"

Lester woke up under a tall cactus, as he covered his eyes to block sunlight, in the middle of a desert. There was nothing on his body than his dirty britches and navy socks.

Dazed and confused, Lester looked to his right and left. He noticed that dry, sandy hills surrounded him.

"What in the hell is going on? Where am I?"

Chapter 3

The Eagle Has Landed

"You have the right to remain silent."

Rhonda was handcuffed and shoved into the back of a police vehicle.

"You stupid tramp!" screamed Gerry as police officers violently restrained him. "You stupid bitch, you killed my girlfriend! You are going to pay for that! What the hell did you do with my friend, Lester? How could you take my truck and go around killing innocent people? You drove over a police officer too! You're going to rot in jail!"

"What are you talking about?" Rhonda was perplexed. She had no idea what happened last night. The confused employee could see that this morning, the green truck had blood splattered all over the front grill, and the tire rims had body parts like fingers and eyeballs tangled in them. All she could remember was drinking and foreplay with Lester.

"They found you in the driver's seat this morning!"

"I am innocent!" cried Rhonda. "I did not do any of this! Why would I drive the truck? Lester drove the truck!"

"Shut the hell up in there!" ordered the cop outside of the squad car. He fiddled with his thick mustache. "That cop you took out was Officer Rowe Manning! He was my partner!"

"Look, officer," reasoned Rhonda, "we had a few drinks last night, and that's all. We had some sex and fell asleep!"

"Then, you killed him!" screamed Gerry. "You killed all these people! You totaled my truck! My girlfriend came to pick me up this morning, and you ran her over in the parking lot! She's dead! Her body parts are all up in my rims and shit!"

"Sir, I need you to step away!" A cop approached Gerry and accompanied his fellows in blue to restrain him. "Did you say this was your truck? Unfortunately, it is not registered. We're going to have to tow it, assuming you do not have car insurance. This whole thing has become fishy. Where were you again?"

"Did I say that was my truck?" Gerry stuttered. "That isn't my truck! What in the hell, cop? I'm out; deuces!"

"You just told her that she totaled your truck, sir."

"You are hearing things, officer! That is my job. That was my girlfriend crushed in the parking lot over there. My friend left with this ho in this truck last night. I never said that this was my truck."

"Sir, you're going to have to come with us too. I heard you say what I heard. Now, turn around and spread your legs. You have the right to remain silent."

"Screw this shit!" Gerry turned around, ran, and pulled out a gun. He didn't want his firearm to go off in his pocket. The police sirens behind grew louder! Police dogs barked like crazy, not too far back.

"Stop in the name of the law!"

Gerry's apron strings got tangled in his feet! He fell over, busted his head on the concrete, and lost his gat in the bushes ahead. He didn't have time to look for it! Instead, Gerry got up and grabbed a branch off the nearest tree. A gang of cops now cornered him, and he was ready to send their asses across the street!

"Put the stick down!" ordered one of the police officers. "I said, put down the stick, boy! You're coming with us."

"Didn't he have a gun earlier?" asked another cop. "I thought I saw him carrying one? So, be careful, sheriff. I'm scared."

"Stay back, cop!" shouted Gerry.

"Do you have a gun on you, boy?" asked the approaching sheriff. "Let me know now so that there are no surprises, and nobody gets hurt. I do expect you to put that stick down by the time I get to you. Do you understand me, boy? Do you under—?

Whack!

"Damn you, boy!" The sheriff absorbed the oncoming branch upside his head from Gerry, cartwheeled off the sidewalk and into bushes, and wiggled his toes through his holy socks because his feet abandoned his boots.

"I told you to stay back, white boy!"

The sheriff screamed at the top of his lungs, "Fire!"

Pop! Pop! Pop! Pop! Pop! Pop!

Gerry was filled with led and launched from the ground! He landed on the other side of the bushes in a dust cloud. As Gerry laid there on his back, his vision faded. He heard the squawk of the ancient eagle and whispered his last earthly words, "Please, take me with you. I don't want peace until there's justice."

The police officers felt a peculiar breeze as if a jet flew over them so fast that they couldn't see it. They almost lost their footing.

Meanwhile, out in the scorching desert, Lester survived. He struggled to walk as shaded areas became scarce! The sun cooked him. There was no water as he talked to himself and beat-boxed to stay focused. His mouth was dry, and his nostrils burned.

Suddenly, hope came upon him for a second. A drop of water fell to his lips! Was it about to rain? No way in hell was that appropriate ever. When he looked up, he realized that the drops of water were nothing more than buzzards' drool. They circled him with vigilance and order, with their eyes on a prize that would fill their tummies and leave enough to carry home to their nests. After all, when Lester divorced, he gained a whopping seventy-five pounds.

The dried ground suddenly trembled, but not because of it finally giving in to his weight. The predators took heed to an unexpected danger that approached from the skies. There was a massive figure that quickly headed in their direction. However, Lester was their meal ticket, so they continued to circle the air above him.

"Wow!" Lester thought. "That is a huge eagle coming this way. That creature is as big as an airplane!"

Indeed, it was not an average-sized eagle, and it was fast! It flew through the circling birds above and sent body pieces of them to Lester's feet. He had to eat and drink to survive, so he made desperate use of the bloody and raw guts.

The eagle landed and stood in front of Lester.

Lester stood up to it. "I hope that you're not planning to eat me. Thank you for this gift of food and drink. These buzzard pieces have saved my life. What is that around your neck? Is that a canteen?

Is there water inside? I also see a box attached to your collar. What's in the box?"

The great eagle stared at Lester with a threatening and sinister gaze. The pupil followed his every movement in its eyeball, but unthreatened, the patriotic bird leaned over and rested its head upon the cracked land.

"Please, don't eat me!" Lester cried his heart out, for he had grown away from his inherited faith. However, time away from his culture brought doubt and forgetfulness to what he faced.

Cautiously, Lester walked towards the patient beast, removed the canteen, and a small box attached to the eagle's leash.

There were bandages, sunscreen, clean shorts, a tee-shirt, flip-flops, and granola bars inside the box. Lester gave thanks to a charitable saint of the desert for the canteen and nearly drowned himself with ice water inside.

The eagle stood up, stepped back, and then flew away. Lester made his voyage in the direction of where the big bird flew. He figured that there had to be a home nearby. After all, the water in the canteen still had ice in it. That bird could not have come from afar!

As the nighttime came about, Lester became uneasy to know that he may not make it to his son's birthday party tonight. Yet, he would lose the trust of his son.

Lester had not seen that eagle for the longest, and there was no sign of any roads. There was one star in the sky, which gave him enough light to cast a view of his hands. He could not see what he walked on, where he pissed, or anything ahead. Most importantly, he had not seen or heard the eagle. All night long, he blindly moved one foot past the other and hoped he hadn't crossed into eternal damnation.

There was suddenly a grasp of hope in his next dreaded step. Could it be? A blue light a few miles ahead, possibly a light, radiated from a television in a house. Lester picked up the pace, and soon after, he reached the light. He cleared his throat.

"Help me! Please? I need help! Help me!"

A burly man in a flannel shirt opened his front door and held up a shotgun. "Who disturbs me?"

Lester stood at the man's fence. "I need help, sir."

"Oh, my goodness, stay right there!" The burly, big man dropped his gun and ran to help Lester. He dragged Lester, who passed out, into his home. "Young man, did you just walk across that desert? How in the hell did you survive that?"

The following morning, Lester awakened to a rooster's cackle. Nestled in a comfortable bed, he kicked his feet to the floor because he realized that he had a party to attend later today.

"Good morning," said the burly man at the kitchen table. He watched Lester come down the stairs in a clean tee shirt and pants he set out for him. "Why don't you have a seat? You've come a long way, so I made you a little breakfast that should help replenish you and give you a little strength for your travel."

"I need to be going."

The burly man laughed. "Where are you going to go? There's not a town for hundreds of miles."

"You're out here," replied Lester. "I'm sure that you're not just living out here in the middle of nowhere. You have to have some sort of something around here."

"No. I am alone. It is what you call witness protection."

"So, nobody can find us?"

"Only certain entities of the government know I'm here."

"So, you're not going to tell me where I'm at?"

"You are somewhere between California and Arizona."

"There's no place between the states. You're either in one or the other."

"Where did you come from?"

"I was in Los Angeles!"

Lester opened the front door and looked out. Then he looked out a window and then another. He stood looking out the back porch door. "I cannot see a thing out there!"

"I live in the middle of nowhere." The burly man fixed him another serving of hotcakes. "Oh, it does exist. It has to. What do you call the area on a map, where the lines divide the states? You are on one of those. That's the best way I can describe where you are now. Go on, sit back down, and join me. I'm interested to know how you got out here. There's no way you walked from Los Angeles!"

"I don't know. I think that I was drunk and driving. Or did I let Rhonda drive because I was too drunk to drive? I blacked out after we made out and drank all that alcohol!"

"For all you know, the broad drove you to the desert and dropped you off. That sounds like a classy woman and some kind of luck. So, let me get my story straight. She got you drunk, rode the bologna pony, dropped you off in the desert, and then she stole your vehicle? I must say that God works in mysterious ways; I'm sure there is a lesson to be learned in all of this."

"Do you have a telephone?"

"No."

"Do you have Internet?"

"No."

"Do you have a vehicle?"

"I am afraid not."

"I do not see a garden. All I see is one annoying rooster. I see that you have a refrigerator and there is a huge meal on the table! How do you get food and mail! I don't even see a mailbox out front."

"The government flies over and drops supplies and food."

"What did you do to end up living like this?"

"That's private," answered the burly man. "I'm not a saint, but if hell weren't real, I'd rather be dead. This shitty place isn't living! The government hid me here; rather, they buried me for my voice."

"Who are you?"

"I'm sorry. How rude of me. You can call me Cliff."

"My name is Lester."

"Lester, it is my pleasure. A lot of people don't usually survive out there on foot. I have not had a live guest in years."

"By the way, do you own a giant eagle? Yesterday, it gave me ice water and food that it had around its neck. It killed a bunch of hungry predators so that I could live!"

"You saw a giant eagle carrying food and water. Then you said it killed buzzards? That had to be a mirage, or I would say that you were either still drunk or hallucinating."

"Not really," said Lester. "An eagle helped, right after it killed some birds that wanted to eat me. That wasn't your eagle?"

"Trust me," answered Cliff, "I do not own any eagles. The only bird I earn is the rooster. And there isn't a home anywhere around here. I swear it! I have been out there, a time or two, in the heat, and hallucinated after some time. Do you want some of this breakfast? Your brain needs it, talking about super eagles and shit."

"I think I'll take a little of the scrambled eggs and grits."

"Sure. Go on, have a seat. Perhaps you can update me on some of the stuff going on out there in the real world."

"I'm sorry, bro. I just don't have all the time in the world. I need to get back out there. Now that I kind of know where I'm at, I've got to try to get to my son!"

"Where exactly is that?"

"I have to get back to Portland, Oregon." Lester chewed down a spoonful of buttery and salted grits. "I need to get there by five today, or I may lose him for good. I'm not referring to the courts, but as a father, because I have broken promises time and time again. It is my son's sixteenth birthday! He's looking forward to me being there. He stays with his mother, and she's talked him into not believing in me. Look at me. I just keep on proving her right. I think this is my last chance, but I'm out here stranded. I tell you, Cliff, life stinks."

"Life throws curve balls sometimes." Cliff licked the sausage grease from his fingers. "I used to be one of this country's great revolutionaries for social change and equality through hip hop, or rather a threat to the establishment, but my family members started to drop like flies the more I sold anti-government rap albums. Before I could lose my wife and children, one of my notorious funding entities, which I cannot ever expose, asked a favor of me that would've sold me out to my people. I couldn't do it. I would not rewrite the wrongs or give such past evil excuses, allowing them to find a painless out for the 400 years of torture to our people. Our people have always forgiven, but every day we're reminded of and will never, therefore, forget."

"I knew that you looked familiar! I know who you are."

"My name is Cliff! Do not say my real name because they have eyes and ears everywhere. As soon as they find out that I have been discovered to be alive by anyone, they'll take my family out. Then they will come for me before the truth of my existence is revealed. They would probably hunt you down as well."

"I won't say your name, but it sucks you have to live like this. You've been reported gone for almost twenty years, man."

"One day, all of this shit will go away. I won't have to stay hidden, but I have to protect my loved ones until that day. I should've never made a deal with the devil. They're very dangerous. Now, I have to live with my choices. But, it isn't half as bad."

"What do you mean? This life has to suck!"

"They see to it that I have plenty of pencils and paper," stated Cliff. He wiped a tear from his cheek. "I have a tape recorder and a basement full of cassettes. All I do is give them some music and trust that my fans will hear me under unreleased music on the Internet."

"How do they get the music if you have no Internet or radio?"

"They allowed me to have a small chopper in the bunker."

"Wait! You have a helicopter?"

"I get in and fly to a specific and approved location about every two months," answered Cliff. "It's heavily monitored. One location I'm allowed to fly into is Canada, and the other is located in Jamaica. There are agents that I meet with, and I give them brand new music."

"So that's how some of those unreleased songs get out there!"

"Yep, they post it as unreleased lyrics on the Internet or get it to underground producers. Those same agents reward me with counseling, women, weed, doctors, dentists, and whatever else. Things have to be this way until I satisfy my punishment for not making such contractual sacrifices, I guess. Maybe in time, they'll let me go; maybe they won't. I took their financial help to get famous, so fuck it. To avoid losing anyone else I care about, this is how it had to go down."

"How do you know your music makes it to the Internet or so?"

"My chopper has a radio in it. Everything is solar charged."

"Do you think that you can fly to Canada today?"

By Ashaki Boelter

"I don't think I have enough songs to warrant it."

Lester stood to Cliff's face. "Don't you have a legacy?"

"Yes. I have fans, to this day, bumping my shit. I've heard the news on the radio about my music. The same thing I rapped about then is the same today, with police brutality and government ills. So, I know my legacy lives on. Life goes on!"

"I have a son," stated Lester. "If I do not get to his party today, I will lose him. My legacy with him is going to be gone. I might as well be here with you and hide, fathering a damn rooster!"

"What do you mean by that?"

"You used to fight!" Lester shouted. "You never hid from any man, and you certainly had no fear of any. You think because you're here that you're helping your family? Have you seen the world today? We're being gunned down, unarmed in the streets, by police. Nobody is being sent to jail for it! Our schools and neighborhoods are not funded to help us! Fathers are less and less involved, as divorce is a common trend for our people now! Do you want to protect your family? I am your family! I can lose my son if I do not show up today! His mother isn't there for him, so if he gives up on me, I lose him to the system! So now, what're you going to do, sit there and continue to rap me a river?"

Cliff, at first, was offended, but then he dropped his head. He cared for and missed his children, just like Lester. The old rapper applied his heart in many songs for their people but left out direct instruction for his children. At that moment, he wondered how they were; he began to shed so many tears.

"Are you okay? I'm sorry, man. I'd mourn with you; I just want to be with my son! Can you please, help me?"

Cliff slowly lifted his head. "Lord knows, you're right. I'm not mad at you. I cannot believe that the dirty game has blinded me! Lester, I should have enough lyrics to warrant a flight to Canada. Lord knows that I don't need a jet blowing me out of the sky. And on the way, you're going to have to jump; they can't know you've seen me. I hope that you're not afraid of heights. I got a parachute."

"What I won't do for love."

Chapter 4

Daddy is Home

"Dad told another lie, didn't he?"

"He sure did," answered Katy. "It is now five o'clock. You have all of your friends here, at least. Now, do you understand why I divorced your stupid dad?"

"Your dad is a loser," commented one of Reggie's schoolmates. "Well, at least your boys are here. Let's start the party!"

Reggie was bummed out, but the party had to go on. "Okay, everybody, let's get in the pool!"

All of the teenagers hopped in the pool in their clothes. Katy turned up the boom box, which bumped 80's R&B dance tunes.

"Dude, the redheaded, sixteen-year-old, is kind of hot," said Johannes. He took a few pictures of her on his cell phone. "I bet she's dirty as hell. She's got a nice butt."

Johannes had a few buddies over as well. They accompanied him at a backyard table, as they played violent dominoes, ate potato chips, and drank beer.

"Aye, Johannes, will you look at those teenage girls!" Johannes's friend smoked a cancer stick. "What the hell constitutes sleaziness today when everything these teenagers wear is simply painted on or up their asses? All I have to say is, thank God for allowing me to live long enough to see it for free! Look at the leggings on that chick, getting out of the water! I mean, she's the size of an average woman! What in the hell are they feeding these girls in high school?"

"Hey guys," said Johannes, "don't tell Katy this, but if she left for the store, I'd probably ask the little redhead cutie over there to come to sit on my lap. And those melons cannot be real at her age!"

"They're real, Johannes! I used to be a doctor!" replied his friend.

Johannes zoomed in with his cell camera. "Maybe you're right? They do seem to move a bit more than fake ones."

"You guys are sick," said another friend at the table. "She's probably sixteen, man! I wouldn't touch that, and it's probably not safe to look."

Johannes looked at that friend. "Brother, we're just messing around. Why are you over there getting offensive about the respect we're giving? Did you go to church on Sunday or something? Man, your old lady has got you tied around her finger and whipped! We can't even look now?"

"Look, Johannes, it's not right. She's just a kid. What if that was your daughter? What would you say to us? I got a sixteen-year-old niece, and she deals with men like you all the time."

"You're right. Okay? Settle down and move out of my way for a second! You are fogging up my phone lens with all that disapproval. I can't tell if it's my camera or your breath, making her ass seemed blurred!"

Johannes's other friends got all excited. "Let us see that picture! She's got a nice booty, but don't forget to get a shot of that blond-haired gal in the tan shorts!"

While the old fellows sat around, Katy stood alert and life-guarded the swimmers.

"I cannot believe that Lester didn't show up," spat Katy. She walked over to Johannes and sat upon his lap. "What is he thinking, to not show up after promising Reggie? He knew this party meant a lot to Reggie."

"Have you tried to reach Lester on his cell?"

"Honey, it goes straight to the voicemail. I have left several messages. Maybe I should be a little concerned, instead?"

"Feel how you want," said Johannes. "I understand. My dad used to pull that shit back when I was young. I'm sure it is hard on Reggie. At least now, you can put closure on Lester being a good father. He isn't good for anything except for child support. You should file for full custody."

Katy made eye contact with Reggie. She suddenly remembered the good in her ex-husband because Reggie strongly resembled Lester.

"What's wrong, baby?" Johannes asked.

Katy stood from his lap and ran into the house. The reality of Lester in trouble or never returning or dead was one that shifted her gears of denouncing his fatherhood.

"Come on, Katy!" Johannes tried to confront her in the bedroom. "Your ex turned off his phone and never had plans to be here in the first place. He's a lousy father and a sack of shit for not showing up!"

"Something is wrong, Johannes. I feel it in my bones!"

"We cannot be up here long," said Johannes. He sat there on the bed and watched Katy stand up. "We need to be down there supervising those teens in the pool. I cannot trust that my friends even know how to swim should they need to rescue somebody."

"Lester, he's so stupid."

"It seems that you're a little stressed to go down there right now," said Johannes. "Perhaps you and I can get down for a sec?"

"Why?" Katy asked, "Did the little girls turn you on, man? I saw you taking pictures, fool. We're going to have to talk about that."

"I was text messaging!" Johannes copped an attitude. "I cannot believe you just accused me of getting excited over some little girls! I wasn't taking any pictures! That's not right, Rhonda. Who do you think you are to be talking to me like that? I'm not your loser ex-husband! You may have talked to him like that, but I'm not the one!"

"I'm sorry," said Katy.

"Katy, you know me better than that!"

"Wait. Whom are you yelling at, Johannes? You had better lower your voice when you talk to me! It is my house, fool!"

"Oh, is that right? Well, I'm the man of the house. I live here! I deserve some respect around here than to be told I am some pervert!"

"Okay! Can we just squash this? It is my son's birthday. We need to get back down there to the pool."

"Not until after you give me a little bit of that coochie. How are you going to accuse me of stuff and get me all worked up and expect me to go down there and be decent?"

"Can you just smoke a cigarette? We need to get down there to watch the kids. We don't have time to get it on."

Johannes wrestled Katy to the bed! "The hell we don't, bitch! I'll be damned to have you tell me what I can and cannot do."

"Get off of me, Johannes!"

"Now listen to me," demanded Johannes. "I am tired of hearing about your on and off caring for your ex-husband! I am the man in your life! How are you going to go back down there, acting all worried about him? I'll be damned to see that happen. Lester is whack! He's the biggest stinking liar and loser on the planet!"

"You are scaring me, Johannes! He's not your problem!"

"Well, he's fucking up my shit around my house!" Johannes reached over and grabbed Katy's arm. He rolled her over to her stomach, and forcefully pulled her pants down to her ankles. "I am going to tear you up! Do you know what I am saying? With all of this arguing and frustration, I need to get some to calm me down!"

"Please, Johannes, don't do this now. My son is right outside with his friends too. I need to be down there at the party!"

Meanwhile, down in the pool, Reggie waded in the water. He watched for his mother to come out of the back door. Instead, his friend Anita appeared.

"Anita!" Reggie swam up to her. "I'm glad you showed up. Did my mother let you in?"

"No," answered Anita. "The front door was unlocked, so I walked in. There was some music coming out of one of the rooms, so maybe that's why nobody heard me ring the doorbell. How are you, Johannes? Happy birthday, big boy, this party looks cool!"

Johannes's friends sat at the nearby table and watched her.

"Hey, dude!" One of Reggie's friends called out from the other end of the pool. "What is that up in the sky? It looks like a big balloon! What is that?"

Reggie looked up at the significant, round figure. "I don't know what that is!"

Johannes's old chums also looked up. "Is it a UFO? It looks like it is getting bigger and bigger!"

Reggie and his friends quickly got out of the pool to admire the odd sight that seemed to grow closer.

Anita asked, "Is that somebody screaming?"

"I hear somebody screaming, but is it coming from the sky?"

"No," answered Anita. "I'm talking about from inside of your house. I thought I heard somebody cry out!"

Reggie shoved Anita out of the way and swiftly ran into his house! He shouted, "Mom! Where are you? Are you okay?"

He ran up the stairs and knocked on her bedroom door.

"Get the hell away from the door!" Johannes threatened. "Your mother and I are taking a little time for ourselves, so go back outside and play with your friends. We'll be out in a second when I'm through with her!"

"Mom, are you okay?" Reggie listened.

Johannes placed his knuckles up to her face. "You'd better say you're okay, or else I'll bust you up. Now you're going to give me some, so get rid of your little bastard."

"I'm fine!" Katy cried. "I'm fine, son!"

"You don't sound okay, mom." Reggie was not convinced.

"Boy!" Johannes shouted. "You get away from that door! We're handling grown folks' business! Thank you!"

Anita walked up the stairs and grabbed Reggie's hand. She whispered, "We probably should go outside. It sounds like they are doing something we probably don't want to be hearing. Come on, and let's go join your other friends."

Suddenly, Johannes's and Reggie's friends started a commotion outside, as they cheered and raised a ruckus! Something big was to come, as the anticipated celebrations grew louder.

Meanwhile, inside the house, Johannes wrestled Katy for some loving. Because the bed springs were so loud, neither one of them heard the cheering.

However, as Johannes gave up trying, he heard a distant yell of a familiar voice outside of their window.

"What is going on out there?" Katy asked as she pulled up her pants and wiped away her tears.

"Where is all of that screaming coming from?" asked Johannes. He stood from the bed and drew the blinds to see outside. "The neighbors are going to call the cops on us if those teenagers don't stinking keep it down!"

Brash! The bedroom window and panes shattered upon contact of enormous hiking boots busting through at a great force!

"Ah!" A man came through the window with a parachute attached. "Oh shit! I made it! I don't believe it!"

"What in the hell is going on here, man?" Johannes stood from the floor. "Who the hell just came through the damn window?"

"Lester!" Katy was severely relieved. She wiped her tears.

Johannes wiped glass from his hair. "What is this fool doing crashing through our bedroom window? I ought to kick your ass!"

"Why is Katy crying, dude?"

"That ain't any of your business," answered Johannes. "She is now an Atlas woman, my wife! I'll do whatever the hell I want with her. Lester, do you see these muscles that I got? Yeah, I dare you to start something. Now, you get your tired ass out of our bedroom!"

"You need to settle down," warned Lester.

Johannes wiped the sweat from his forehead. "We'll discuss how you'll pay for our window in a bit, trying to be a superhero or something. Fool, you aren't shit! Now get out of here, so I can finish having rough sex with your ex-wife! I'm hard as hell."

Lester looked at Katy. She was scared.

"I think she needs to be downstairs with her son," said Lester. "It is his birthday. You two can do all that, another time. It is Reggie's time now. Come on downstairs and join us at the party."

"Man, you have five seconds to get your ass out of my business!" Johannes popped his knuckles. "Nobody let you in my house in the first place, and it would be simple to beat you down like an intruder and call the cops."

Katy's eyes bulged with more tears and redness. She shook her head for Lester not to leave but feared that he was not reliable ever and could never be genuinely counted on for much.

"That's it," stated Reggie. He watched Lester turn around and head out of the bedroom. "Take your sellout ass out of our bedroom and enjoy your son's birthday party in the backyard. Go eat some cake and ice cream, you stupid asshole."

Lester felt an uncomfortable ache in his leg from the crash landing as he carefully limped down the stairs. He heard the bedroom door slam and kept on. Lester figured that Katy made her bed, and now, she could lie in it. He was there for his son.

"Son, I made it!"

Reggie was so happy to see his father and jumped into his arms. He tightly hugged his father! "Everyone, this is my dad! Dad, this here is Anita! Isn't she hot?"

"Oh," replied Lester, "she's a lovely, young woman. You've got the same taste in women as your father."

Anita blushed and shook Lester's hand. Then the other kids, who'd never met Reggie's dad, followed.

"That was neat, sir, how you came down out of the sky," commented one of the teens. "I wish my dad would do some cool shit like that; that was awesome!"

"Who are those old, gangster guys over there playing dominoes?" Lester pointed to the table.

"Those are Johannes's friends."

"Excuse me," said Lester. "I'll come back to hang with you in a minute, son. I need to ask them something."

Lester casually strutted over to Johannes's friends' table. "Excuse me, guys. I am the boy's father. Listen, gentlemen, do you know what's going on upstairs?"

"Why should any of us know?" One of Johannes's friends cackled. He had missing teeth, and his breath stunk. "They're grown."

"You guys can't hear Katy and Johannes screaming out the window? Isn't that inappropriate during this party?"

The drunk responded, "Man, haven't you ever had sex before? That's what folks do when they're humping, and it gets good. They scream their heads off. It's on you that the damn window has done' fell off from crashing into the house. You can hear them now!"

"Excuse me for a second." Lester marched into the house and stomped up the stairs. It was not the time for the couple to do that.

"He's what?" Johannes answered his cell phone. One of his homeboys in the backyard called to warn him. "He's coming up right now? That fool is asking to get his ass kicked! Doesn't he know that I will wear his old ass out? He's coming up right now?"

Boom! Lester kicked open the bedroom door!

"Get your filthy hands off of her!" screamed Lester. He dove onto Johannes, who zipped up his pants!

Lester swung like mad and bloodied Johannes's lip, but Johannes doubled up right jabs, and Lester soon had meat hanging off his face! His face bled from several cracks in his cheeks and a split eyelid.

Reggie ran into the bedroom, grabbed his mother by her hand as she covered herself with the bedsheet, and ran her downstairs

As Johannes beat the mess out of Lester, Reggie called the police. Meanwhile, all of Johannes's friends rushed out the front door, to their cars, and off down the street.

Suddenly, Lester rolled down the stairs. Reggie continued to punch away at Lester.

"Get off of my dad!" Reggie shouted as he and his friends jumped on Johannes's back! "Get off of my dad!"

"What?" Johannes was out of control. He body-slammed a teenager through an end table and tossed another kid into a record player. "You little shits had better get off of me, or else I'll kick all of your asses too!"

"Stop hitting my dad!" Reggie kicked and swung at Johannes's head. *Paft! Paft! Paft! Pow!*

Johannes stopped swinging and stood up straight. He pulled Johannes off his back. "Are you going to stand with this loser? I don't care if he donated sperm to make you. I am a real man! I am the one who is raising you! He's never come through for you! He calls himself a father, but you have never been able to trust his word. He's all talk! He has never treated you that good!"

"I hate you, Johannes!" Reggie jumped at Johannes with a haymaker! He missed and caught an uppercut from Johannes! His friends were shocked and backed away from Reggie's stepdad.

Police sirens neared as Johannes continued to pound away on Lester's face with his bloody fists.

"Thank God you're here!" Katy pointed to her husband and ex-husband as a gang of cops marched into Johannes's melee.

Johannes screamed out as he was restrained. The cops arrested him and dragged him out of the house to a squad car. "Katy! You tell those cops about what's up! Your ex-husband intruded on your son's birthday party! You tell them that, damn it! You tell them that!"

An ambulance showed up, and the responders assisted Lester. His nose was broken, his lips hung like tomatoes, each of his eyes looked like two hotdogs, blood streaming from his forehead, and he talked gibberish.

"Tell them about that jerk!" Johannes hollered from the back seat of the squad car. "That man is crazy! I was only protecting my family! I'm the good guy! I'm not the bad guy!"

Reggie shouted at his mother, "You tell the police what happened! Mom, what are you doing? Say something! That's dad over there all busted up because of you!"

Katy glanced at Lester on the stretcher. That bloodied man did not have to stand up for her; he could've stayed in the backyard and did nothing. She'd forgotten about the kind of man her ex-husband was for such a long time, and she realized again that he truly loved her through his most significant flaws.

Lester had always been a protector and a decent father. Katy fell into her fellow employees' set-up, where her friends suggested she get a divorce and start over with a man who had money. Johannes may have had money and a big peter, but Lester always held Katy's heart with friendship. She tried to disgrace him for years to justify her decision to leave, but sometimes, love just would not let go.

She felt supremely sorry about everything she had put Lester through. She then wondered if she could have him again. Would he even take her back after all she had done to him?

"Ma'am, can you tell us what happened?" A cop stood in front of Katy and awaited a report. It was time to stand on the right side of history, to keep her son safe from now on. "Ma'am, do you want to press charges?"

Chapter 5

Ruining a Legacy

"What is going on here? My ex-wife decided not to press charges, so why are you detaining me? What gives? I think that I need a lawyer!"

"Lester Hairston, we would like to know where you were last night." The Portland Police Department's Detective Barnes and Detective Burnside circled Lester in a small room. There was a table in the center, under a tiny light fixture, where Lester sat. Along the upper corner of the far wall was a small window, opposite the privacy mirror, so the room was not completely dark.

"What is this? What is going on? I should be a free man! I rescued Katy from domestic abuse, and this is how you thank me?"

"You are not a free man," stated Burnside. "I beg to differ! What we want to know is where you were last night!"

"I was in Los Angeles."

"What were you doing in Los Angeles?"

"I was at my company dinner accepting the Employee of the Year honor. Why do you ask? What are you detaining me for?"

"Do you know a Rhonda Patterson?"

"I know of her. Why do you ask?"

"We found her yesterday morning in a green truck that we believe belonged to a man named Gerry Moses from Warm Springs."

"So?"

"The truck was used last night for a killing spree," said Detective Burnside. "We found Rhonda getting out of that truck, which was covered with blood from running down individuals."

"Did she run over Gerry or something?"

"She is still being questioned. However, we caught up to Gerry, and he resisted arrest. He picked up a stick and nearly took the head off of one of the officers. Well, that did not end okay for Gerry. He was gunned down, and he did not make it."

"What in the hell did the cops do that for?"

"We are sorry for your loss."

"Fuck you! He was my best friend, you bastards!"

"The truck, at some point before midnight, was used to strike Gerry's girlfriend in the parking lot, and it killed her. There was a security officer on a cigarette break at the casino, and apparently, the truck mowed him over too. There were several cars in the parking lot that were also struck."

"We didn't do all that, but those cars were barely nicked!"

"So, you were driving the truck?"

"Wait for a second!" Lester halted. "What the hell is going on here? Are you guys from some kind of candid television show? Are you punking me? What the hell is going on here? We had a little alcohol, but we didn't do all of that! We nicked a couple of cars at most!"

Suddenly, in the small window, the very same eagle in the desert peeked into the room. Of course, the only one that noticed the big bird eye was Lester.

"Were you driving the truck, sir? Don't let me ask it again."

"We had a few drinks, and that's all."

"Who had a few drinks?"

"Rhonda and I had a few drinks, but I swear that I woke up in the desert! I did not smash into anybody! Look, if you think I'm crazy, how do you explain the eagle standing outside that window?"

The detectives turned to look, but the eagle wasn't there.

"Sir, I don't know what kind of meds you may be taking, but we need you to focus!" Detective Burnside was impatient. "We want answers! What happened last night?"

"You know," answered Lester, "I was taking Rhonda to her hotel, but we kind of took a detour. We parked at a rest stop. What do you want to know next, officers? I released the Kraken or slapped sloppies! And as far as I can remember, we stayed there for the night because we passed out with all the drinking and tiredness."

"Go on. What happened next?"

"We snored? I probably farted a few times; I do that often."

"You don't recall Rhonda or yourself driving back to the casino's parking lot, mowing down people?"

"I told you! I was asleep!"

"Then where did you wake up? All we found was Rhonda."

"I woke up in a desert that was far away from Los Angeles."

Detective Burnside shook his head. "Come on, man."

"I woke up in a desert with just my underwear and socks on!"

"How did you get back to Portland? How did you survive in the desert? It's sweltering down there at this time of the year."

"An eagle showed up when I was on my last leg and fed me granola bars and water. It gave me survival supplies."

Detective Barnes yelled, "Come on, man! What do you take us for, some idiots? Are you saying for the record that an eagle came out of nowhere and helped you with supplies so that you can make it across the desert? You're killing me, man! Get the hell out of here!"

"That's what happened, sir. I swear it!"

"Then, where did you go?" Detective Burnside asked.

"I found my way to this guy's house. His name was Cliff. He looked a lot like Santa Claus. He housed me until the morning and then flew me to Portland in his helicopter. I parachuted onto my ex's house, hence the parachute it the bedroom."

"Well, that's a fact," said Detective Barnes. "We did find the parachute, and the teens said you came down from the sky. Tell us more about this Cliff guy."

"He's in a witness protection situation under the Feds, and he is not able to be found. What does that have to do with your investigation in the Los Angeles deaths?"

"We ask the questions," warned Detective Burnside.

"So," reiterated Detective Barnes, "you made it through the desert and stayed a night with a stranger named Cliff, who looked like Santa Claus, and nobody can find him because the government is hiding him. Then he happened to have a helicopter and flew you to

Portland? Man! That is the biggest crock of shit we've heard all day! I cannot take this. Can somebody get me a stinking aspirin?"

"Hold on!" Detective Burnside tapped his chin. "There was a military patch on the parachute."

"That's because it belonged to the government that keeps Cliff hidden from the rest of the world," said Lester.

Detective Burnside asked, "Did he tell you why he's hidden?"

"That's a matter of National Security," said Lester.

"What the fuck?" Detective Barnes threw up his arms. "This idiot is delusional! We should hook this guy up to a lie detector test immediately. I want the truth about who killed those people!"

"All I know is that I did not kill anyone," added Lester.

"How would you remember what you did, being wasted?" Detective Burnside angrily added. "We know that you drove that truck at some points, as we have fingerprints on the steering wheel. Rhonda said that you knew Gerry. Another employee witnessed you and Gerry arguing in the restroom before the company meeting about religion. You and Gerry went to the same high school, so maybe there is something in your past that came to light? I don't quite have a motive yet, but there is something you are not telling us."

Lester was tired of the questioning. He was tired of fighting Katy. He was tired of struggling to represent his culture while he was becoming successful at work. Gerry wasn't the only person that called him a sellout. He wanted to be his own man, at anyone else's expense. His faith was based on the eagle that said he could fly above all. This police episode was a hinder, while his faith guided him to rise.

"Are you looking for motives?" Lester asked. "You said that Gerry's girlfriend showed up and that she was picking him up since I had his truck."

"Go on."

Lester continued. "Was she pregnant, or did she have a child?"

"They did," answered Detective Burnside. "They have a three-year-old together."

"Gerry told me earlier in the night that he never paid child support. He did not have a girlfriend. So, why else would she come to his job to see him?"

"Keep going. We're listening."

The eagle angrily stared into the room at Lester.

"Well, isn't that a motive? Gerry has several kids and baby mommas. He told me that he would never pay any child support to any woman! Wouldn't it make sense to try and look at this for face value? Maybe we did leave the rest stop and may be returned to the casino? Maybe Gerry got in the truck and smashed the baby momma. He's always had a temper. Maybe the security officer happened to be in the wrong place at the wrong time? He did smack the shit out of a cop with a branch. All I know is that I woke up in the desert."

"It seems like you are pointing the finger at your friend Gerry," said Detective Barnes. "You're kind of throwing him under the bus. We hadn't heard many negative things about him from his fellow kitchen staff at the casino. They thought he was very nice."

The giant eagle outside the window had flames in its eyes and stared with extreme anger at Lester.

"He was ignoring his responsibilities!" Lester sat up in his chair. "There he was, purposely working one part-time job and hardly caring about making more and more children. I told him that child support pushed me to find a better and higher paying job to take care of my kid. Maybe I finally triggered something in him by being honored by such a company, which I remind you that he also worked for before me. He quit because of racial pressures, while I have excelled through that and achieved a great reward of being the Employee of the Year. I think he's the killer, and you killed him."

"Wow. You make it seem like Gerry was a real loser."

"It makes sense," said Detective Burnside. "I'm still curious about the fellow in the desert, however. Also, if your friend, Gerry, really had it in for you, why wouldn't he have put Rhonda in the desert and sat your drunken ass behind the wheel? Don't you think that it would've been simpler to pin you for these crimes? We believe you drove the vehicle, but video from the casino parking lot was not functional to show us who truly drove the truck."

"And as far as the guy in the desert, he blindfolded me until we got miles away from his home. So, I do not know his location. I'll tell you what I do know. Gerry hated America and was a womanizer. You have to look at things for face value."

The detectives scribbled notes.

"I'm sorry," continued Lester. "Did I mention that our conversations had a lot to do with police hatred? So, if you're looking for anybody that hates the police, he's your guy. I love police officers! Can you fellows give me a ride home after this? Katy's house was a closer walk to my place."

Detective Burnside put away his pencil and pad. "We thank you for your cooperation, and we'll be in touch. As far as your car, it was transported here from Los Angeles, and now it sits in our yard."

"I cannot thank you guys for everything."

"The front counter will have your keys and costs."

"Thank you, guys. I'm glad that we cleared up a lot today. As you can tell, I'm not the bad guy here."

"Have a nice day," said Detective Barnes.

The ferocious eagle in the window trembled with complete rage at Lester. After all, it, or he, a spiritual godhead of his divine religion, that kept Lester alive in the desert and inspired him to give cultural and faithful recognition. Was this his shining moment? The eagle thought not. At that moment, the Employee of the Year, a once-proud family member of the Tenino people, was nothing more than a two-faced, lying, and targeted sell-out.

The fact was that a drunken Rhonda drove the truck away from the rest stop as Lester slept off his swollen gonads in the back during the middle of that night. A few hours, Lester's got out to take a leak on the side of the road. Drunk still, Rhonda drove off and left him in the desert.

She drove back to the casino, used GPS, but could not map out pedestrians in the parking lot. She left a bloody mess of the entire situation.

Unfortunately, Gerry's girlfriend was in the wrong place at the wrong time. She only visited his job to demand child support. The security officer was simply smoking a cigarette under a tree when he walked over to address the commotion. Gerry returned inside the casino to see if he could get an advance, so he missed the security officer consoling the crying mother minutes later.

That is when the green truck mowed them over in the lot and spun into a dark area away from the front doors. The green truck's engine was loaded with so many guts that it came to a sudden mechanical halt that flipped Rhonda upside down in her seat. The officials found the vehicle in the morning. Gerry hadn't a clue.

Gerry had room to grow, as every man has at some point. The only legacy building for Gerry now was a nasty police record that included assault and murder; that did not sit well with his lingering spirit. What would his kids think about his life? He had seen them from time and had mailed gifts without return addresses yearly. He just wanted to be a hardcore gangster when it came to his friends, as his life journey trained him to be, but underneath, he tried.

However, Gerry's bastard train grew long and now spilled over the hill! It was recorded that he didn't pay child support, and then he ran over some people in a lime-green truck with a camper on the back! It was all a lie.

That did not fly with the heavens of indigenous people. According to the original land's ghostly forefathers, things had to happen if somebody ripped away your legacy based on lies or an ego.

It flew away, an eagle with great wrath and focus. Lester's heartbeat echoed throughout the universe. He should not have told lies about his resting friend and ruined his legacy; he had been warned earlier about the truth.

Chapter 6

Confrontations

"It seems like forever since we've gone to a movie, Katy."

"Lester, you do like extra butter on your popcorn?"

"You know it," answered Lester. He grabbed Katy's hand and kissed the back of it. "Don't forget about the red licorice. I'll be back. I have to go to the bathroom. Use this twenty-dollar bill."

"Um… That is not going to cover the cost. It's the 2020's."

"That's not enough for popcorn and a small drink?"

"Where have you been, Lester? The treats will cost at least twenty- five dollars. Thank you. I'll be waiting for you when you come out."

Lester was proud to have reconciled with his ex-wife. He truly loved her, and the first thing he established with her was that he was not putting up with a mouthy woman. No more fighting and arguing, creeping and cheating, no more lying and bashing, because he did not have it. No more yap yapping. She was either in or out. Lester had always willed to be with her forever.

Counseling, on top of medical testing, was in session. Katy promised to be on the same page. She wanted her man back for good, and she was truly and honestly sorry.

It was their first date in months. Lester had that old strut back, and he walked into the men's john. Oddly enough, there was nobody there. He walked up to a urinal, unzipped his pants, aimed, let out a giraffe fart, and let the juices flow down the urinal.

While he stood there and punished the porcelain with the digested coffee stench, he heard a stall door creek. As he wiggled his ding-a-ling to finish the drops, he looked over his shoulder. "Oh shit!"

Quickly, Lester zipped up his pants and backed out of the bathroom. He couldn't wash his hands because what stood in front of the sink was that ominous and enormous eagle from the police precinct and the desert! It stood at least ten feet tall and stared at him with rage. Lester fell into its haunting eyes and heard a war dance song accompanied by many tortured screams of criminals burning in snapping flames. There was nothing friendly about its confrontation this time, as it stooped over to fit inside the john. Lester sprinted past that eagle and into the theatre lobby.

"There's a gigantic bird in the men's bathroom!" Lester shouted and grabbed the theatre manager to check it out.

"Are you sure what you saw was an eagle?"

"I saw it with my own eyes, man!"

Katy left the food counter line and asked, "Are you feeling okay, Lester? We don't have to see this movie. I know we've been through a lot. We can just kick it at my place, you know. Reggie is staying over at his friend's house tonight, so we have some private time to get it in."

"Maybe, we should get on home." It had been forever since he had a piece of Katy, and she always had a banging body.

One of Katy's work friends happened to also be there on a date.

"Hey, girl," greeted the work friend. "Where is Johannes? I see that you have a new one. Who is this handsome man?"

"He's my ex-husband." Katy looked at Lester and smiled.

"It is a pleasure to meet you," said Lester. He extended his hand to shake the friend's hand. "And you are?"

The friend looked pretty stupid about now, but she reluctantly extended her hand to shake his. "He's your ex-husband? Well, I am Shirley. Um, Katy, what in the hell is going on here? I thought you got over this man?"

"Let me tell you something," answered Katy. "You may think you know me, but you don't know him. So, all the advice you gave me could not be fair to him. You only had one side of the story. I was going through some things that didn't involve him too. I shouldn't have listened to any of you at work. You ladies weren't real friends!"

"Oh my goodness, it sounds like he brainwashed you, girl!"

"No, he didn't," said Katy. "He's my best friend and takes care of our son too. Lester will not have me doing things I don't like to do, like smoking weed in front of my son and hanging out with many losers who like to take pictures of little girls. More importantly, he's not going to bust me upside my head every week! This man has always loved me, and I am going to treat him right from now on. You and the rest can stay out of my business. I cannot believe that I even called you, my friends!"

"I guess. I mean, this fool isn't all that. You're so ugly."

"What?" Lester was appalled. "Look at you!"

"What about me, bitch?" Shirley popped her from side to side. "At least I ain't skinny like you, looking like you use dental floss to wipe your narrow ass!"

"I got this, baby," Katy reassured and stepped up.

"Katy, I did a lot to get you hooked up with Johannes!" Shirley looked at Lester and puckered her lips. "Ewe, I can't believe you gave up a bedroom god for this malnutrition weasel?"

"What exactly did you do with Johannes to get me hooked up with him, Shirley?" Katy wanted to know. "I know you did something. Did you pay him some money? Did you sleep with him like I expect everyone at our workplace did? It's a shame that Johannes lives like he's all that because women like us create these monsters by giving in to his bull jive."

"You had a choice, sister," Shirley stated. "You're the one who willingly pleased him. You know, at first, nobody thought he would swing it your way, but then he inquired about how come you were off-limits. To be honest, we all thought there was no chance you'd give it up to another man, being married and all, but you can thank Lester for that. He wasn't enough for you then, and I can sure as hell tell, meeting him today, that he isn't enough for you now. Once you go, Johannes, you don't go back to this!"

"Oh, I get it," said Katy. "There was a bet?"

"That's right. We bet that if Johannes couldn't get some of you, he wasn't as good as he claimed, and we would spread it all over town. However, if he won, which he did, we'd give him some money and a week full of more than enough booty."

"You made a fool out of me? Lester is the father of my son, and a decent enough of a man, Shirley! How could you?"

"Again, you decided to open your legs for Johannes," said Shirley. "We did not force you to do that! And once he got some, he was so into your goods that he decided to hang up his game. Girl, he loved your body! He bragged a lot that your husband's thing must be micro-tiny because he thought you felt like an adult virgin! He told us all how you screamed in pleasure and nearly broke out of the handcuffs you wore the first time."

"That's enough!" Lester was appalled by Shirley.

"Whatever, man, you weak-ass fool with a small penis," replied Shirley. "Now, Katy, you go on and live your pathetic life with that boring man. I've got better things to do. And when you see me at work, just keep on walking by. I do not associate with women who are losers. Bye."

"You're old news!" Katy shouted.

"You all look pathetic and sick," said Shirley, who walked away. "Just wait until Monday when I return to work! I'm telling everybody about how stupid you are, Katy. That ex of yours is weak and nerdy. Good luck with that!"

"That was rude," commented Lester, as he and Katy watched Shirley exit the lobby.

"I'm sorry," said the lady behind the concession stand register, "but did I just hear that Johannes is free? Who doesn't know Johannes? He's only the hottest man on the planet! I need to sign off for a break and give him a call for a date!"

The maintenance man overheard the concession stand employee. He dropped his broom and excitedly dashed to his janitor's office and dialed Johannes for a date, too.

Later, to keep his mind off of what just happened, Johannes leaned into Katy and watched the movie previews. Lester's nerves were jumpy after the confrontation with Shirley, and more about what happened in the men's bathroom.

"Why did you seem all jittery after you left the men's bathroom?" Katy recalled.

Lester answered, "You wouldn't believe me if I told you."

"Try me."

"There was a giant eagle in the bathroom."

As Katy chuckled, Lester pulled out a sandwich bag with blue pills and wondered if those made him delusional.

"You use those nowadays?" Katy asked. Then she chuckled. "I guess whatever gets the job done, right? However, are you taking too many? Maybe that's why you see eagles and all. Can you drive?"

"Of course, I can."

"Well, drive me in your golden chariot to my lair, king."

Hours later, back at Katy's house, the two sat on the couch and relearned one another's body. They were indeed desperate for one another as they fondled and groped each other right out of their clothes. When they tipped the loveseat over, they both knew it was time to take it upstairs to the boom-boom room with the hole in the wall where the window used to be.

Katy slowly trotted up the stairs with Lester in pursuit as his drooling tongue wagged, and he steadily watched her familiar jiggly, visibly panty-swallowing, and meaty booty move side-to-side.

Lester and Katy dived onto the king-size bed, which had newly fresh sheets. All of the foreplay happened downstairs, so this was all business. Slickened and moist, the desire was there, and that made it simple to enter with effortless comfort. Love was in the air as they rolled with starving crocodile tears in a river that busted through a damn and flooded the bedding.

Katy flipped her back into a ponytail and rolled Lester onto his back. She nearly pushed him through the box spring, as she was already near her first lift-off. The countdown was set to blast off to the moon. The rocket man began to tremble as a sudden buzz overtook his booty muscles. Katy put her back to avoid whiplash and strapped into the sheets. The countdown began! 5-4-3…

"…Two and one, and we have a lift-off!" Katy screamed.

"Here we go! That's what I'm talking about, Katy!"

"I'm flying!" Katy shouted. "I can soar, and I can weave! And more so, I am not even trying! I'm…! My goodness, that was great!"

"Katy, did you just try to sing—?"

"You've got me hooked! Doing this again with you is like a happy fairytale ending! You're making my dreams come true."

"Who said I was done? I just need a little water and an ice pack; I'll be back to it in an hour."

Katy grabbed Lester's tee shirt, put it on, caught the breeze coming through the hole in the wall, showed off her figure in the moonlight, and then she headed downstairs to the kitchen.

Lester climbed under sheets, as his damp skin caught a chill. He thought, "I missed that body." He was so satisfied that nothing else mattered. He listened to Katy, who grabbed things from the refrigerator. Then, he heard her walk into the restroom.

Suddenly, the bedroom became darker. Lester rolled over and expected that the moon disappeared into a typical Portland rain cloud. The bedroom door violently slammed shut on its own!

"What in the world!" Lester jumped from the bed and ran to the bedroom door. He struggled to open it! He turned towards the hole in the wall and justifiably screamed, "What do you want from me, you stupid bird! Stay the hell away from me!"

The enormous eagle sat in the backyard. It was so tall that it stared through the hole in the second-story bedroom wall.

"Ah!" Lester screamed, opened the bedroom door, and sprinted down the stairs. He looked back up those stairs and saw the tip of the eagle's beak leaving the bedroom! Lester turned around and banged on the downstairs bathroom door!

"What the hell is wrong with you?" Katy cracked open the bathroom door as her dookie fumes shot out. "I am in the middle of taking a huge dump! Do you mind, Lester?"

"I'm sorry, but there is a giant eagle in your house!"

"I think you need to see a shrink, or you've got a blue pill drug addiction. Do you hear yourself? What are you talking about?"

"That eagle is following me! It found me!"

"The one that you claimed was in the theatre bathroom?" Katy asked. "Have you lost your mind?"

"Yes, and maybe, I have!"

"We'll talk about this when I'm done," said Katy.

"No!" Lester busted into the bathroom and slammed the door. He locked it. "It is after me!"

"We cannot stay in this bathroom all night." Katy wiped and flushed. "How can you stand the smell in here? I dropped doozies!"

"It is the least of my problems! Okay?"

"You are welcomed to sleep here for the night," said Katy, "but I am getting out of this bathroom right now. I am going to open this door. Then I am going to bed and going to sleep. Move out of my way, Lester. You are tripping."

Katy opened the door and casually walked up the stairs. Lester carefully and cautiously followed.

"Good night," stated Katy. She seductively climbed into bed and turned over. "Lester, you try to get some sleep. I'd like to get it in the morning, too, if you're still not eagled tripping out."

Lester slithered with fear into the bed and nervously pulled the sheets over his head. He curled into an embryo and slept under Katy's soft breasts. He felt safe for the time being, but sooner or later, he would have to face his lawful eagle's wrath.

Chapter 7

Egotistic

The next morning, Lester woke up to the delicious smells of buttery eggs, bacon, sausage, and buttermilk pancakes with crisp edges! Katy was downstairs in the kitchen, cooking breakfast the way she knew her man liked his food: Greasy, buttery, and flavorful.

The sun radiated through the bedroom hole in the wall. Lester stretched and yawned in his old bed. He knew that he'd done it right last night to have his ex-wife in the kitchen cooking a tasty breakfast. He was the man again!

Lester suddenly heard his cell phone, which was in his pants pocket on the couch, downstairs. It could not have been his job, as they gave him a paid month off after being named the Employee of the Month. Plus, they wanted the murderous situation handled and boiled over before he was allowed back.

When Lester looked at the caller ID on his cell, there was a Los Angeles area code on it. It was probably important; perhaps the LAPD called him about an investigation on the truck murders.

"Hello?"

"Hello, is this Lester Hairston?"

"Who is asking?"

"This is Detective Barnes."

"How are you doing, sir. It is Lester speaking."

"Mr. Hairston, I called to tell you that there is not going to be a trial or case. As you probably know, I came down here to Los Angeles to help with the investigation, and we've got witnesses and tourists that have come forward with personal video. It clearly shows a drunken Rhonda erratically driving alone in the lime-green truck."

"I'm an honest man," said Lester. "I'm a respectable person, and you guys should've trusted me from the start."

"Aren't you confident today?" The detective flicked the tip of his nose. "Anyways, your story jells that you were not in the vehicle. We have secured a video of her also dropping you off outside of town. Rhonda has been convicted."

"She wasn't worth my time."

The detective was unimpressed. "You have one nasty ego, you arrogant asshole. Against my every being, we would investigate a conspiracy to kill, but we have no motive or connection that concerns you with the slain individuals. It turns out that you just met Rhonda."

"Well, she met me. She wanted some, and I delivered."

Detective Barnes aimed to finish his call. "And I don't know what you came in counter within the desert, besides delusions, but it is of no concern to us per the US government, as you have safely made it home. We have been instructed to drop the case with you. So, congratulations, I believe you're a free man. Goodbye."

"Ha! Ha!" Lester hung up the phone with delight. "I'm free!"

"What are you celebrating?" Katy asked.

"Oh, just some unfinished business that is finally over. It smells so good in here!"

"Just a little something-something I put together for my baby. It's ready now. So, Reggie said he would be home around noon. This request may be a little weird or different, coming from me, but can we get at it one more time before breakfast? I just figured we wouldn't reveal how much we're into each other physically with the boy until later. Can we get one more episode up in here?"

Lester picked Katy up in his arms and carried her to the laundry closet. He dropped her on the washing machine and turned it on to the spin cycle! There was too much clothing in the machine, so it was unbalanced and banged all over the place. The lovers shifted their hips to avoid broken bones and from sliding off into another room. Lester's knees dented up the washing machine's steel front, while Katy's heels dribbled off of his drizzling and muscular booty.

"Hold on!" Lester shouted.

Katy wrapped her arms around her ex-husband and squeezed him so hard that everything embarrassingly came out of his body, from zits to chromosomes, to spit and gas! As the washing machine ended the cycle, she and her man plopped-over one another like two slabs of raw pizza dough.

Later that afternoon, Reggie returned home. He was so happy to see his biological father and mother sitting on the couch watching television. It was like the old days. "Hi everybody, I'm home."

"Hi, son," greeted Lester. "I didn't hear you come in. How was your friend's house?"

"It was cool, dad. We went on a double date last night."

"You were with Anita?"

"Yep, I sure was."

"She seems like a nice girl."

Katy was left out in the left field. "Excuse me, but how is it that I don't know about Anita? Who is Anita?"

"She's my girlfriend, mom."

"Oh no, she isn't," said Katy. "You cannot date yet."

"What? Are you kidding, mom?"

"You are not responsible enough," added Katy. "You don't do chores around the house as I ask, your grades are sloppy, and you watch too much television! You're not dating until you're eighteen."

"Mom, are you insane?"

"Boy, you'd better watch your mouth before I smack it!"

"Hold on!" Lester stepped between mom and son. "If I may say since I am his father, add that I think he is ready to date. Katy, from what I've seen of him and Anita, he's game. Plus, now that he's got a real man in his daily life that will focus on him, I can teach him how to treat a woman. Katy, I know that I've been absent, but I am guessing that Johannes corrupted his little mind. Katy, let me take a swing at this. I owe it to this family."

"So, what are you saying? He's okay to date?"

Lester stood to his son and put his arm on the boy's shoulder. "Katy, let's just invite the girl over for dinner and go from there. Maybe we can escort them on dates until we both feel they are ready. Can we at least start there? I wasn't named the Employee of the Year for no reason; I must make pretty good decisions. And my son believes I'm an excellent father. Will you start by supporting my decisions? Aren't I the man of the house now?"

Katy hesitated. She bit her tongue. "Okay, we'll start there."

"You're cool with that, mom?" Reggie was excited. "Oh gee, mom, that's awesome! I'll invite Anita over tomorrow for dinner. Thank you, mom and dad, for allowing me to date. I'll go and call Anita to see if she's free right now! You're the man, dad!"

"Not before you clean your room!" Katy shouted.

Reggie sprinted up the stairs and closed himself in his bedroom. Lester shrugged his shoulders and dusted off his hands.

"You did overstep my rules, and don't let it happen again," warned Katy. "Next time, let's talk about things first. I know you feel that you've won everything, but check your ego around here."

"Oh, you know I'm right." Lester led Anita back to the couch. He kissed her on the neck and caressed her breasts until she submitted.

"It looks like things are going to be very different around here, and for the better, I hope." Katy chuckled because she was ticklish, not because of his sky-rocketed ego.

"It's already better, Katy."

A commercial came on the television from Harry's Eagle Car Insurance, the insurance that beat many price quotes from top insurance companies across the country! Lester jumped when the commercial ended with the head of a bald eagle that covered every inch on the television monitor!

"I need to get back to my house," said Lester. "I almost forgot that I have plants to take care of and a bird I need to feed."

"I didn't know that you had a bird. Since when did you get into birds? What kind of bird do you have?"

"I have a gigantic bird. It might be a canary or something."

"Canaries are not that big. You don't know what kind of bird?"

"I guess not. I'm bird blind, perhaps."

"I almost forgot that you didn't live here, Lester," said Katy. "I have missed you so much! I missed making love to you. What we did last night and this morning was incredible! It wasn't all violent and gross; it was smooth and tender. Fate has us in its eyes."

In the back of Lester's mind, he wasn't fooled by fate or a quick fix with Katy. His ex-wife had chased waterfalls like Johannes while she was married, and she almost drowned. Now that Lester caught her with a lifesaver, he wasn't about to pull her aboard that fast.

Lester had forgiven her, but he had not forgotten how she treated him while she was with Johannes.

Katy had to wade in deep water for a bit with sharks until she got all attitude out of her system, as far as Lester was concerned. He felt a little Johannes residue spat on his winning ego when he mentioned teaching his son about dating women.

"Hey, dad, are you leaving?" Reggie hollered as he grabbed a vacuum from the upstairs closet.

"I have to take care of things at home, and I'll be back."

"Can we have dinner tonight like the old days?"

"That sounds great, Reggie!" Katy cheesed. She looked at Lester. "Are you down with that?"

"You're not cooking, are you? I'm just kidding."

"Don't start," laughed Katy. "I hope six is good?"

Everybody agreed. Katy and Reggie saw Lester off.

When Lester returned to his home, he immediately turned off the house alarm. He strutted to the kitchen, grabbed a wine cooler from the fridge, spun off the top, and took a sip.

"Oh man, I smell like sex," Lester said to himself. "I cannot believe where I'm at with Katy, but Lord knows, I'll take it. She is freaking hot! I got to take a shower."

So, Lester took a quick shower and finished off his wine cooler. After he got dressed and packed a bag of overnight clothes, he placed the alcohol bottle in the recycle box underneath his kitchen sink.

Lester headed to the front door with his bag of clothes. He punched in the code for the house alarm to start and opened the door.

Rawk! The mighty eagle stood at his doorstep! It had dark shadows underneath its piercing yellow eyes! Drool drizzled down from its beak, which looked like a giant hook you'd find on an excavator in a construction site! The enormous bird flapped its wings, which expanded past Lester's peripheral vision!

"Ah!" Lester slammed the front door, and a screw dropped from the door hinge! He thought, "I knew that it would show up here! I'll just let the house alarm go off and watch the police gun it down."

He looked through the keyhole. The eagle patiently sat.

"I cannot believe nobody sees this monster at my door. When the cops blow it away, I'm going to fry that son of a bitch and chew the hell out of it. That thing does not know who I am! I'm Lester Hairston, for goodness sakes! Nobody or nothing messes with me!"

Rawk! Rawk! The eagle pecked on the door even harder. *Tick-tick-tick! Tick-tick! Tick-tick-tick!*

Suddenly, the house alarm sounded. Lester turned off the alarm, and as he anticipated, his cell phone rang.

"Hello? Yes, I require the assistance of the police. There is a burglar! My code is 5-5-5-5, and my place of birth is Vacaville. I don't have time for questions! You hurry up and dispatch the police! They're in the house, but I'm hiding. Do you want my name? My name is Lester Hairston, the Employee of the Year, and the king of sex! What? Have I lost my mind? What? Nope, I am not conceited, and I don't have an ego that large! Get me your manager! Hello? Hello? No, you didn't just hang up on me!"

Suddenly, there was a knock at the door. Lester opened it. He expected the police, but it wasn't.

"Who are you? Where are the police?"

"Dude," said the United Freight package carrier on his doorstep, "I just want to deliver this package to Lester Hairston. I believe this is the correct address."

"Yeah, it's me."

"I need you to sign here. And thank you."

"Wait. Did you see a giant bird out here, about ten feet tall? It was just out there! How in the hell could you miss it?"

The alarm company representative heard that and hung up. They labeled the signal as a false alarm. "Dude is on crack."

The freight delivery carrier shared the same sentiment about Lester. "Have a nice day, sir. You might consider seeing a shrink."

"Whatever." Lester received a package from his job, another piece of their appreciation. Just as the egomaniac turned away from the carrier, a dark shadow covered the corner of his box!

Rawk!

"Ah!" The United Freight package carrier waved his arms for his life as the eagle levitated above the doorstep. It tried to lift the package carrier from the ground by his head with its beak, but the guy had an enormous ass from all the long hours in the delivery truck. So, the eagle ate his head. Then it inhaled the rest of his body!

Lester backed away the front door as the eagle landed and threw its head back to jiggle the carrier's body of moving nerves down its throat. Then it flew straight up into the clouds above.

Lester ran to the kitchen window at the opposite end of the living room and looked back towards the front door.

Suddenly, his neighbor Ted walked up to his front door. "Hey there, Lester, what is up with the mess on your doorstep? Did you leave these tennis shoes out here? They're messy with all the red paint, but if you clean them up, you could sell these bad boys online."

"Ted! That's blood on those shoes!" Lester shouted. "Please, go home! Get away from there!"

"What's gotten into you, Lester? I just wanted to come by and see how your trip to Los Angeles went."

"You must go home, right now! Listen to me!"

"Do you have a woman in there? Is that what's going on?"

"Do you not see the giant bird out there?"

"I see a couple of crows on the telephone wires? Why? Let me in, buddy. I promise that I'm not going to push you to come to my church this Sunday. Look, Ethel, and I wanted to congratulate you on the reward you expected to receive with this case of beer."

"I sure could use one of those! Get in here quickly!"

"What're you so shaken up about, Lester? You're acting as if you'd seen a ghost or something? How was the trip to Los Angeles? Did you just get home? Is everything okay?"

"Yeah, okay, everything is fine."

"Then why were the cops over at my house the other day asking questions about you?" Ted opened a beer.

"The cops came to your place?"

Ted took a sip and replied, "They asked questions about your character. So, you tell me what's going on."

"I lost a good friend the other day," answered Lester. "A drunk driver of his truck ran down some folks. I was in the truck before it happened, but I got dropped off prior. I had nothing to do with all that. Do I seem like a person that would do all that? I'm Lester Hairston!"

Ted wasn't sold, from Lester's jittery or ego trip. "I think I should go on home. You seem a little off, on-edge, and perhaps you need space to think about all that."

"What do you mean by that, Ted? You think I did the crime?"

Ted walked to the front door.

Rawk!

"What in tarnation was that sound?"

"You cannot leave, Ted! It'll kill you!"

Ted looked at Lester. "What? Now look, friend, you're acting a bit strange for my liking. I'm leaving, and that's it."

Rawk!

"Ted, do not open that door," said Lester. "There is a large eagle out there that wants to kill me, and it'll kill anyone in its way."

"That's the dumbest thing I've ever heard."

"Take a peek out the front window, man!"

"Oh shit, man, what the hell!" Ted stepped away from the blinds. "Man, what in the world did you do to get a giant eagle, like that, at your front door?"

"I don't know. It's been stalking me all over the place since I got back to Portland. It's eating people around me!"

"Well, it ain't from around here! You had to have done something to get it mad! Where did you first see it?"

"I saw it in a desert, somewhere between California and Arizona a few nights ago. However, it helped me survive. It could've killed me then, but it didn't. I don't know what I did to get it angry!"

"Are you sure that it is the same bird?"

"It is."

"Well, you must've got it mad somehow." Ted looked directly into Lester's eyes. "You have to think back. From what I know, you've been to jail, and it waited. You didn't return home, that I could tell, because I watched over your house, until today. It never showed up while you were gone."

"I don't remember what I could've done… No, I can't."

"You said that pretty slow as if you have an idea."

Lester puckered his lips. "I remember a story that Gerry, my good friend from high school, who was shot down in Lost Angeles, last telling me of our Native faith."

"What exactly did your friend say, man?"

"Ted, it was only a fairytale."

"And so are the eagle and those bloody sneakers on your doorstep! Now, spit it out!"

Lester began. "Gerry said something about how white settlers tried to take our ancestors' land and how a giant eagle came up and killed the settlers with their guns. The Giant Eagle supposedly still protects the hard-earned legacies of those Native Americans of lineage, even in death. If anyone tries to disrespect the dead's land or legacies, they'll deal with the Great Eagle. To Gerry, that was his interpretation of our faith. It wasn't my truth of the Great Eagle, so I took his as entertainment and fantasy. There's no way that garbage is true!"

"That enormous eagle has to be after you because it is protecting someone's legacy then," said Ted. "Did you perhaps say something to a girlfriend or co-worker or even the cops to hurt Gerry's reputation or legacy?"

Lester answered, "I don't think so. All I told the cops, who were pointing the finger at me for a fatal hit-and-run accident at the time, was that if they wanted a motive for who the driver could be, they *should* consider Gerry. Not only was it his truck, but he told me how messed up he was, not paying child support and making babies without being responsible for his doings. He lived his life like a sperm donor and was a slut! His truck was filled with drinks, drugs, and condoms. He used to work where I worked, but he pissed away the opportunity by turning ghetto on a very conservative corporation. He quit his job and skipped town to impregnate more women. As a childhood friend, he was cool, but he was a slut and a disgrace to our people as an adult! He had the nerve to preach to me about truth?"

Rawk!

"I think that you just answered your problem. That bird is protecting Gerry's legacy, or it is a reincarnation of him in some kind of supernatural way. Either way, it's coming for you, Lester."

Lester dropped his beer can. He couldn't drink. "That would explain why it helped me in the desert."

"What do you mean?"

"The eagle is a manifestation of Gerry's soul," celebrated Lester. Then he shook his head in disgrace. "That means that I royally messed up; he spoke of the truth. I have been brainwashed by society's ills and disowned my traditional teachings. And do you know why? I took my teachings and catered them to my liking; I believed it as truth, instead of the real truth that Gerry preached."

Ted added, "And from the sound of it, you wouldn't listen to him when it mattered. You got that award for Employee of the Year, and your head got bigger."

"I got my son and ex-wife back and immediately tried to make rules in their home." Lester recognized that he was out of control. "I was cocky when I spoke the police and ripped Gerry's legacy apart. I am truly eagle tripping out; it cannot be true!"

Ted looked at his cell. He was going to call the police. "Why is the coverage for my cell phone not picking up in your house all of a sudden? That's never happened!"

Lester looked at his cell phone, and his, too, did not pick up reception. There was no landline.

"Do you have a gun, Lester?"

Lester shook his head no. "We have plenty of knives! It's two versus one, and we can cut it up. What do you say?"

"If it goes airborne, it gets the advantage." Ted thought up a plan. "You can distract it from the backyard, and I'll run out the front door and go home to get my gun. Then it is open season!"

"That's a great idea!" Lester sprinted to the backdoor. With a kitchen knife, he stood in the backyard and looked on the roof. "Hey bird, I'm back here! Come to my back porch!"

Whud! The eagle flew upon the rooftop and slowly walked towards the backyard. *Clit-clack. Clit-clack. Clit clack.*

"There you are, you big stupid bird!"

Rawk! The eagle's eyes turned blood red as it drooled from its beak and cautiously walked towards Lester from the roof.

"Come on, you stupid bird. Come on!"

Clank!

"Oh no, I think I busted my leg!" Ted shouted because he accidentally tripped over a bloody sneaker at Lester's front door, and his knee landed on a sprinkler head!

"Run!" screamed Lester. "It heard you!"

The eagle raised an eyebrow and lifted off from the roof in a complete U-turn! It dove from the rooftop towards the front door!

"Blahh!" cried Ted. He couldn't move fast enough. "No!"

"Ted!" Lester stormed back inside his house and rushed to the front door with his kitchen knife. He opened the front door!

"Ah!" Ted swung his fists, miserably missing the eagle. His lungs got jack-hammered by the eagle's beak, similar to forking the plastic wrap on a meatloaf TV dinner before putting it in the microwave. His lungs protruded out like buttery worms.

"Ted!" Lester ran to help his neighbor, but after one swing of the knife and the eagle snapping at him, he ran back into his house and slammed the front door shut. Lester sat there in the window and watched the eagle pull and pop veins from Ted's dead body.

Rawk!

After the enormous eagle finished gnawing on Ted, it flew into the sky with his crappy intestines that hung out the side of its beak.

Lester could not bear it anymore! Unlike the package carrier, Ted's blood was splattered all over the front door, his roof, the bushes, and the walkway.

Knock-knock-knock!

Eagle Tripping Out

Lester looked into the peephole on the front door to see who knocked on his front door? The last person he wanted to see at his door showed up; it was Katy! He slipped the kitchen knife into his pants pocket and immediately opened the front door.

"Hey, Lester, what're you up to?"

"What're you doing here, Katy? You need to get back into your car and leave here now! I told you that I was coming back."

"Why are you telling me to leave? Our son went to the neighbors to help with yard work. I thought you and I could get a little freaky before you come by tonight for dinner."

"You need to turn around and go home, Katy."

"What's wrong with you? Do you have some chick living up in your house or something? Why are you tripping?"

The enormous eagle landed behind Katy and licked its chops!

"Don't you see all the blood on the ground and walls?" Lester pointed to the eagle behind her. "Slowly turn and look behind you!"

"You're starting to scare me, Lester." Katy looked around as the eagle maneuvered, not to be seen. "Oh, is that it? Do you have a United Freight carrier chick in your house? No, I won't leave! See, I just got off the phone with one of my girls, and *she thought* it was a good idea for me to stop by your place to see how you are living. And wouldn't you know? You won't even invite me inside. I don't hear any canaries either. For all I know, you could be raising a child the same age as our son. So, what's going on here, brother?"

"You don't see the blood all over the place?"

"No, I don't see any. What blood?"

"It's all over the bushes and the ground! Look at those sneakers by your feet. Do you see the blood all over them?"

"Man, I don't know what kinds of medication you've been taking lately, or if the sex pill is too high of a dose, but the sex we had must've shaken some screws loose in your head! Those are a very nice clean pair of sneakers on the ground. Are they yours?"

The eagle had quietly tip-toed right up to Katy with its beak wide open! Lester could feel and smell the eagle's breath, as it was close enough to eat Katy."

Lester quickly snatched his ex-wife by the arm and yanked her into his house before the eagle beaks slammed shut!

Slam!

"Damn!" Katy was on the floor after being flung by Lester. "What is your problem? Why did you toss me to the floor, man?"

Lester looked through the peephole, but there was no sign of the eagle. "I'm sorry, Katy! I don't know what's going on with me."

"I don't either, but what's up with the knife in your pocket? You know that I'm always packing a piece. I wouldn't want to pop a cap in your ass, so you'd better put your knife over there! Go on!"

Suddenly, they heard the carrier's truck start out front. Lester placed the knife on the kitchen table. He returned to the front window and watched the package carrier, who got eaten up minutes ago, drive away! Then, there went Ted, who walked his dog past his house!

"I am completely losing my mind!" Lester shouted. "I swear that the Great Eagle killed them!"

"You're still talking about that eagle? Is this the same bird that you said was at my house?"

"You've got to believe me, Katy! It is trying to eat me!"

"You need to get help as soon as possible. You're tripping."

"I saw it eat the package carrier and the neighbor! My entire house was painted in their blood! The sneakers were bloodied!"

"Calm down," Katy instructed. "Look, if anyone knows you, it would be me. That's what scares me. I can usually tell when you're lying. You're not lying. You truly believe what you saw."

"Yes!"

"There's no blood, and the carrier just drove away."

"Oh, come off of it," said Lester. "You know that you don't believe me. That's why you're looking at me like that. And you don't trust me; that's why you're here in the first place. You're always listening to your friends. You came over here to see if I had a female in here."

"That's crazy and untrue! I came over here because I couldn't stand another minute being away from you! We have a lot to work on, and I'm willing to start from scratch."

"So would I!" Lester shouted. "But, I don't want your friends all up in our business. That is how it all started. That is how Johannes ended up in the picture. I am the same man as before, but I'm willing to change. I need you to be patient and committed. We cannot have you being one foot in and one foot out in our relationship!"

"Okay, I get it. I was wrong. Is that what you need to hear?"

"Yes!"

"Well, there you go." However, Katy wasn't done. "But, listen to me when I say that you're not the same damn man as before. Since you became this 'Employee of the Year,' you've been an egotistic, eagle maniac, and a chauvinistic pig!"

"How dare you talk to me like that?"

"Why am I not allowed speaking the truth?"

"I am Lester Hairston, and I will not ever hear of such talk in my house by a woman! I'm the man! Do you got' that?"

Rawk!

Knock-knock. There was a knock at the front door.

Katy walked towards the back door as she spoke. "Look, Lester, I need what's best for our son. I was wrong to cheat with Johannes and destroy our marriage and friendship. Our son didn't respect me for my decisions. However, as soon as you returned to the picture, I can see that he is a better person! I know that he needs you. I need you! I am sorry, and I hope you can forgive me. And please, drop the tough-guy, egotistic attitude."

"I don't have an ego!"

Rawk!

Knock-knock-knock.

"Wait, Katy." Lester begged, "Please, do not open that door."

"Why?" Katy sarcastically smiled. She puckered her lips. "Is it because you came home for her? Are you afraid that I'm going to open this door, and some bitch that you've been with is going to walk in here? I will not be played, Lester!"

"Katy, you've got to stop listening to your friends!"

"We will see about that when I open this door!" Katy snapped her thumbs and grabbed the front door handle. "I ain't some fool."

"You're crazy if you open that door!"

Katy looked through the peephole. "Oh, you're after the older persuasion these days? She's got pretty silky white hair. Well, she's going to have to take her social security-having ass back to the convalescent home when I get done with her!"

"Don't open that door!" Lester shouted.

"The hell I won't!" Katy pulled out her gun. "Lester, stay your ass over there by the kitchen! I got something for her ass. You should've been honest with me, sitting there humping me all night and morning at my house. What kind of fool do you take me for?"

Katy aggressively opened the door and realized, right then, that when she looked through the peephole, she was looking at the back of an eagle's head in the peephole! The enormous eagle turned around to look dead at her in the doorway.

"Lester!" Katy screamed. "What in the world is going on here? You did see a giant bird. I'm sorry that I didn't trust you."

Lester grabbed the knife from the kitchen and warned Katy to be still. "Any movement may provoke that monster."

"Look how it's looking at me," said Katy. She cocked the trigger on her gun. She looked down at the ground. "Oh my goodness, Lester, I can see the blood!"

"Can you trust me now, Katy?"

"Yes!"

"If this eagle is the spirit in which Gerry spoke of, maybe I can reason with it? Let's try to be calm about this!"

"What are you talking about?" Katy shouted at Lester. "You think this animal understands English? Are you crazy?"

"You can't trust me, Katy?"

"I'm not sure," said Katy. "You're not the same man, who I once trusted. Right now, I don't even want to deal with all that. I have to defend myself before I get eaten!"

"Katy, don't do it!"

"Eat lead, you ugly eagle!"

However, the enormous eagle was faster than Katy. Like a powerful vacuum cleaner, the eagle inhaled Katy to the back of its throat! Then, she slid further down into its throat until her forehead sizzled in its stomach acid! Her legs wildly flailed from the eagle's smacking beak. *Crunch! Crunch! Gargle! Crunch!*

Lester pulled at his ex-wife's legs, but he couldn't hold on because her urine and defecate smeared her legs into an oily disaster! His heroic hands slipped away as he swatted at flies and then fell to the ground with his ego crushed.

The eagle threw its head way back, and the rest of Katy slid down its hatch like humongous snot.

Gulp. Rawk! Burp!

A pair of Katy's granny panties, her wedding ring that Lester purchased, and her car keys sifted from the eagle's drooling beak and landed on his doorstep.

"You killed my girl!" Lester screamed at the eagle. "She was the queen of my life! You've messed up now! I am going to be your greatest nightmare, you stupid bird! I have faced far worse than you, serving in wars! Therefore, I am a proven winner! You can call me Lester Hairston, and I'm coming to get you for this!"

Rawk?

"I am the man, and if you have anything to do with Gerry," said Lester, "you're going to regret messing with a real winner! You're a fowl and a flying rodent of the planet! If you're not on my plate, fried, with a side of mash potatoes and a biscuit in the next day, then my name isn't Lester Hairston!"

Rawk! Rawk! Rawk!

The eagle angrily shot into the clouds above and swooped downwards in the direction of Katy's home, a few blocks away.

"Oh, no, you won't have my kid, you son of a bitch!" Lester picked up Katy's keys and made a mad dash for her tiny car. He jumped in, started it up, and wore the tires out, headed for Katy's place. "I have got to get my son out of there!"

Chapter 8

Ego Mania

Lester threw his cellphone, which had no signal, over his shoulder, and slammed on the brakes of his ex-wife's car. He made a mad dash to Katy's front door of her house!

Blast! He kicked the door in and looked for his son. "Reggie! Are you here? Son, get down here now!"

As he searched the quiet house, Lester remembered that Katy mentioned Reggie was helping out next door. Lester quickly turned around and headed to the front door.

Slam! The front door blasted shut. Lester pulled the kitchen knife from his pocket that he brought from home.

"Hey, dad, it was horrible!" Reggie slid into the kitchen as he tried to catch his breath and wipe his tears. "A giant eagle, the size of a whale, swooped down into my neighbor's backyard and ate my friend's parents! Then, it ate Anita and two of her friends, dad! We were just helping with the grass and weeds when suddenly it swooped down and started killing us! What're we going to do? The phones don't work!"

"We're going to kill it!" Lester shouted. He held up his kitchen knife. "That's what we're going to do! Where is it now?"

Reggie paused. "Wait. Where's mom? Is my mother here? Mom, are you upstairs? Lester, where is she?"

"Nobody is going to get us," said Lester. He pulled his son to his body and hugged him. "You can bank on that!"

"Did it get my mother?" Reggie ran upstairs and looked for his mother. "Hey, mom, are you up here?"

Knock-knock-knock!

Lester carefully looked through the peephole. "Gerry?"

Gerry stood on the outside of the front door, as clear as day.

"Open up!" Gerry demanded. "If you want all of this to end, then you must open this door!"

"How do I know you won't try something?"

"How long have we been friends?"

Lester angrily flung the front door open. "I should cut you into pieces with this knife and burn your parts to hell! Nobody messes with Lester Hairston and gets away with it! Do you know who I am and what I've been able to accomplish here?"

"Lester, I don't believe you know who you are," replied Gerry. "I think you've lost who you are in your daily situations. You've become egotistic and are benefiting from your closest allies' reputations. I was your best friend, and after what you said to the police, I will darken the rest of your journey!"

"You unforgiving ghost-piece-of-shit, do you know who I am?" Lester began to sweat. "I am Lester Hairston! I have always worked harder than you. I've always achieved more! So, your way of bringing me to the misery you had, isn't going to work. I've always been better than you!"

Gerry chuckled. "Your godly ego does not match your absent legacy. When you leave earth, the only person who will remember you for who you are is your son. Nobody sees you as you see yourself. Would you like me to read off the list of what people see of you? You're selfish, you bash your closest friends and adversaries, and you're a sell-out—"

"Stop right there!"

"Most people have left something that benefits somebody," said Gerry, "even if they were not of the same background as you. I would not have known it, but people do turn over in their grave when they're supposed to be resting in peace."

"Zombies are real?"

Gerry clarified, "No, they're not literally turning in the graveyard, but wherever they are, they still are sickened at living people like you. Did you know that when you got that job, and I left, you never called me once? When I met you in Los Angeles, you made sure to point out how low of a person I was because I didn't pay child support. You didn't know my struggle, Lester! You judged me as if you're God. Your ego went through the roof when it came to me. No man on this planet is equal to the creator, so the rest of us are of the same grain, born of sin and fighting to make life right. I told you about the truth of knocking somebody else down! Well, now, doesn't it hurt? You're losing the ones you love, left and right."

"First of all," explained Lester, "I am not a sellout! I got a job that most minorities can't handle. I worked my ass off through all the same racism you worked through. I stayed and fought it! I also fought for my son and his mother to be back in my life. Do not tell me that I am not myself. You know how much of a fighter I am! I haven't changed!"

"I beg to differ."

"Gerry, you've given up like the poorest people of my interpretation. You've done very little for work than striving for part-time work and counting on government assistance. You run from your baby mommas' and hope they raise your child right. Your legacy, I wouldn't know, but from what I see, it is garbage. The way you profess, you almost sound like you are the Great Eagle."

Gerry sinisterly smiled and looked past Lester. "Maybe I should have studied our entire faith to understand the whole truth. Perhaps you're right that the entire truth would be discovered not within one teaching but as a whole after it is has been studied from a distance. Am I the eagle, or does the eagle even judge? Or do I request the eagle, while the eagle is simply a vehicle to carry out God's instruction? Or, is the eagle an incarnation of God or the Devil?"

"Dad, help me!" Upstairs, Reggie screamed for his life because the giant eagle extended its head into Katy's room. Her son knelt, looking for his mother under the bed when the eagle's sharp beak trapped his leg!

"Well, obviously, Lester, I'm standing here with you." Gerry laughed as he watched Lester sprint up the stairs to his son.

"No!" cried Lester. He charged at the eagle with his knife as it circled the room with his son. "Give me back my son!"

Rawk! The eagle tossed Reggie into its throat! *Gulp! Crunch-crunch. Gulp! Rawk!*

"No!" screamed Lester.

Brash! The eagle stormed out the hole in the wall, but scrubbed some of the wood, and sent a blinding blizzard of wood fragments and nails to Lester's face.

Lester watched the eagle fly away into the sky. The beast sprinkled his son's blood all over the fences and trees as it disappeared into the clouds.

"You bastard, I'm going to kill you!" Lester was mentally gone. He ran back downstairs to face Gerry.

Gerry stood at the door and smiled. "What're you going to do? I'm already dead, fool. I wonder who else I can torture you with killing. Are your mother and father still alive? I want you to suffer for the rest of your life! Help me and tell me, who do you have left?"

Suddenly, a figure stood behind Gerry, as he quickly disappeared into thin air.

"Honey, I didn't know that you'd come back so soon." It was Katy at the front door. She stepped over the kicked-in door and said, "Well, Lester, if you didn't have a key anymore, you should've called me and asked me to make one. I just left the store to buy a bag of potatoes."

"Katy?"

"Lester, I hope it isn't too expensive for you to fix my door." She walked to the kitchen and emptied her grocery bag. "You are going to fix my door, brother. And I guess by now, you know our son isn't here. He's next door helping with some yard work. I just checked on him, and he said he'll be there for a few more hours. Do you know what we can do in a few hours? Let's try it in the shower!"

Lester rubbed his eyes. "Katy, did you see Gerry?"

"Honey, maybe we shouldn't have sex that often. Your mind is still shaken up from this morning. Perhaps you should take a nap?"

Lester dropped his head. "What is going on?"

"Honey, come here and hug me. It's a lot to swallow right now with the changes. I love you."

"I'm not going to keep going through this torture," whispered Lester. The gruesome and bloody images in his head outweighed his current reality. "Katy, I need to leave."

"You need to fix my door, bro."

"I love you, Katy," said Lester. "I could never live in this world without you. The moment you left me, I died. It broke me too much. Right now, with all of this that I'm going through, I feel nothing more than a dead man walking. Take care of my son, because if Gerry could do it and still be, then so shall I, as it is of the truth."

"Wait!" Katy shouted as she watched Lester head out the front door. "You'd better not walk out on us! Lester! Come back!"

"I did the best I could do," said Lester. Suddenly, he saw that his car was where he parked it last night after the movie date. He reached into his vehicle and found his key hidden under his seat. "I got to go. Goodbye, Katy."

"What in the hell, Lester, don't leave us now! You're scaring me! Come back here!"

Lester sped away from that he saw the eagle fly away. He turned on his stereo and searched for music to calm his nerves.

"Boy, you're learning a lot today," said Gerry. He suddenly appeared in the passenger seat! "I'm glad for you to recognize that you're not a better man than the next man. Men live to dominate and rule. That's what a man is. We read God's language and interpret it to our use and empowerment. I see that now you're coming to your senses. You're no better than me, asshole."

Lester turned up the stereo.

"You need to hear me out," warned Gerry.

"You are just a ghost. Preach to your own' congregation that believes everything and every word you say without question."

"I said everything based on our teaching. You can't question our faith! It's the truth!"

"What human doesn't ask questions or is told they cannot ask questions and shuts up? Oh, that would be you, and men like you. We were given brains to study beliefs as we live them. We weren't just given one-track minds to only sit and record. Teachers allow questions, while dictators tell you to put your hands down and to shut up. And if you ask or have a different way to the same answer, you get labeled a backslider, a heathen, a sinner, or a liar because your life was not done the same way."

"You sound confused!"

"I am not confused," replied Lester. "I am free. I am free to question the truth to find the absolute. I am an individual who was created in God's likeness and was given specific gifts and traits to use. I have a brain and a specific journey, unlike yours or anyone! So, kick rocks if you're going to say your truth is the only one, even though a million interpreters are saying the same thing you're saying that they are speaking the truth. I'll let you know the truth when I find it. So far, you're a big fat lie. So, if you're going to roll with me, Gerry, can you please shut the hell up?"

"I am going to haunt you for the rest of your life!" Gerry screamed. "I'm going to find everyone you know and torture you!"

"You sure have a big ego, being dead and all, Gerry."

"No, I don't."

"Gerry, what do you think your kids are going to think of you when they grow up, you piece of trash. They're not even going to care. You wasted your life doing nothing. That's the truth! You were a low down, lazy, no-good player that lived your life in lies. I'm surprised that you're not burning in hell."

Gerry steamed in the passenger seat. "You're so dead, Lester!"

At a distance, Lester saw the enormous eagle in the sky. "Oh no, I think I made somebody else mad. Here comes the eagle."

"You should've been talking about me!"

Suddenly, Lester smashed the accelerator pedal with his foot and drove through many barricades and warning signs about the bridge being closed due to not being complete.

"What are you doing, Lester?"

"I'd rather die a winner with a great legacy, whereas everyone knows I tried my best. Did you leave this world with that behind you? You can go to hell with all that haunting me for the rest of my life. That isn't going to happen!"

"Lester, you need to settle down and turn the car around."

"I will not!" Lester shouted as his old car caught 120 miles per hour. "Here's a truth about the matter at hand. When I make the afterlife, you had better run and hide because I'll be looking for you. Gerry, your ass is mines!"

Gerry stopped talking and began to fade away.

"Oh, okay, you'd better run!" Lester tore through the last warning sign, and his car flew into the sky, nearly one hundred feet above the ground! Lester opened the car door and jumped for the eagle, which soared above. "I got you, you stupid bird!"

Rawk!

The eagle exploded into a cloud of mystical clouds and glitter as Lester and his old car fell into endless rocks below. The entire area exploded into a fiery mushroom cloud of machine and guts.

There stood Gerry, feet away from the explosion and smoke. He looked at the awful accident and said, "Well, Lester, now you've done it. You have killed yourself. That's an even greater legacy for your kid than mines. Reggie's dad was a suicide artist. That's great."

"Are you talking about my legacy?" Lester laughed as he stood from the explosion and walked towards Gerry. "You have been ego-tripping from the beginning of time, making baby after baby, with women. You were then turning around, bragging about how you don't pay child support and who was next in line. What a life! Nobody will remember your name, and that's an ego downer."

"Screw you, Lester! I hate you, man!"

"You're already forgotten in the real world. The truth is that life is about what you make of it and preparing for the afterlife. Life is about sharing and growing. Life is about loving. Love is taking care of your responsibilities when it comes to your woman and your kid. You didn't do any of that. You failed, player! I may have ego tripped, but in all of that, I spoke the truth about you."

"I don't need a lecture."

"Well, Gerry, that means then that it is time to get your butt kicked. That is what's up."

"You cannot fight me in front of heaven's gate!" Gerry hysterically laughed. "You're a loser, Lester! What are you going to do now? I dare you to throw a punch in front of God's house!"

Lester put a hurting on Gerry in a tremendous spiritual battle. He flung Gerry around heaven's gate, and the angels had a hard time separating the two. Lester didn't care about being judged at the moment.

Eagle Tripping Out

"All men are born being short to the glory of God. Well, here I am, Lester Berry Hairston! I accept what happens to me!"

Gerry chuckled as he limped and soothed his swollen eyelids. "Lester, I hope you go to hell! Not only are you violent, but you also committed suicide! Ha-ha! I know that you claim Christianity since you married that ghetto woman in Portland. So, your truth is that all Christians go to hell for committing suicide. Somebody press the button and send Lester to hell!"

An angel of light stood in front of Lester. In that light, to the left of, the Great Eagle perched upon heaven's gate. The angel spoke, "Lester Berry Hairston, you have been revived on earth, as God commands it. It is not your time. Go with peace, and enjoy your life with your family. Clean up your act, however, and we hope to see you again many years from now."

"What?" Gerry was angry. "He killed himself! How in the world can he go back? Plus, his car fell 100 feet off a bridge! There's no way he could've survived that! He doesn't even know or practice the truth! He spoke terrible of me after death! That's not right!"

The angel looked at Gerry. "His words were true of you. They were not lies. I believe you're saying that he should tell lies about you when that is unacceptable to do."

"So then… What about me? Send me back too!"

"You're a selfish, egotistical, dead-beat dad, womanizing quitter. How many children did you make? So, that's twelve times for the same sin of disrespecting women."

"I've accomplished good things too! Just ask the Great Eagle."

"I'm sorry," said the light, "but the eagle is an animal. It cannot speak human. Do you think we don't see everything? You wasted your life on purpose and never walked the talk or teaching."

"What about my religious tattoo? I have spiritual qualities! I dressed modestly! I sang all of the church songs growing up!"

"You're not going back, Gerry."

"Alright, fine," said Gerry. "Let's just go on into heaven. I'm sick of arguing with you, angel. I just want to be somewhere. I got here and got beat up by Lester, and now you're stalling me."

"Gerry, you are not welcomed up here," said the angel.

"Then, where am I supposed to go, fool?" Gerry stood back and puckered with attitude and disgust. "Huh? I need bandages and ice for these bruises! Where do I go? Do you know anything, lit up angel whatever-thing? How'd you get that job in the first place? Huh? Lester killed himself, and I was shot up! He's supposed to go to hell because he committed suicide! I know that's in the bible! How does that make sense, fool? Are you going to let that fool go back? You know he'll go back, repent and turn his life around to get in heaven! It isn't fair! You're not doing your job. I'm not with this bull jive, angel! You're going to play favorites now?"

Suddenly, Lester disappeared. He was returned to life on Earth to spend with his son, to better his experience with faith and restoration. God had indeed worked in mysterious ways. Nor did he need to give a reason for his judgment, the ultimate judge of life.

"Where the hell did Lester go? You sent him back, didn't you! That's some bull jive. You crack-head angel!"

"Gerry."

"Don't you Gerry me, mister angel! I should be walking through those gates right now! No, you shut your mouth, angel! Don't you interrupt me; do you understand?" Gerry was animated with his hands. "Go and get me your manager or somebody that knows what they're saying! You're nothing like the angels that I've read about in teachings. You don't deserve those stinking wings! And who are you to tell me where to go? I'll hop this damn fence if I have to and suck up all the heavenly accolades on the other side! Do you know who I am? Huh? If you don't know, you'd better ask the giant ass eagle, fool! Yeah. What's my name, Great Eagle? Say it, bird!"

"You have eagle-tripped out for the last time. The eagle cannot speak, for the last time! Goodbye, Gerry. You can get your hand out of my face! Gerry, I'm not kidding."

"Whatever, you stupid angel and bird can stuff it!" Gerry held his middle fingers to the perched eagle's face also.

"Gerry, you're a piece of work."

"Look at me!" Gerry laughed. "I'm giving the bird to a bird, chicken shit! I get the last laugh up in this mug!"

A distant horn sounded. The note was quite depressing.

"God has judged you, Gerry. It is time for your exit."

"Fool, please, I'm not going anywhere!"

"You're going to hell."

"Yeah, right," said Gerry. "Man, God is not mean. He'll have something to say on this. God has a huge heart! He loves everyone, and he won't hurt me or anybody. He's not like any judge we have in the world, a bunch of mean, hard-hearted and soulless goons with a gavel. God would excuse a speeding ticket and let a killer free because he loves us all! Praise the Lord! Forgive me! See, I repented and now I'm good to go! Now, step aside you giant fire fly."

"You do know that God is the ultimate judge, right? God is not just a toll manager or a traffic director. You're either in or out with God. And according to what I've been directed to do here, you need to back up and get to stepping, dude."

"You can move your glowing and half naked behind out the way, angel! I'm going through those golden gates. Move it, sucka'!"

"Goodbye."

Click. The floor beneath Gerry opened, and down he went into the fiery pit, where his skin melted off his face, born someone and ended as nothing.

By Ashaki Boelter

Eagle Tripping Out

By Ashaki Boelter

978-1-7358905-3-1

www.ingramcontent.com/pod-product-compliance
Lightning Source LLC
Chambersburg PA
CBHW060436260626
47161CB00005B/1951